DUEL IN THE SUN . . .

Slocum turned to Mire. "You ain't all that bad. But you're bad enough."

Mire smiled. "Yeah, Slocum. Reckon I'm bad."

The two men faced eath other in the dying sun.

Slocum studied Mire. He could see no fear. Mire had won too many gunfights and wasn't nervous now. He expected to win. Slocum felt keyed up. He was facing a top gunfighter, one of the best.

Slocum knew the signal trick in the eyes, when the brain gave the command to move. He studied Mire, aware that Mire, too, watched him with fierce intensity.

Nobody moved, the sky flamed, the grass swayed in the breeze. Then Slocum saw it, the eye flicker.

They both moved, a brilliant display of top gunfighters at their best—smooth, perfect, no waste, all speed.

They both went for their guns. . . .

OTHER BOOKS BY JAKE LOGAN

JAKE LOGAN

SLOCUM AND THE
TRAIL OF DEATH

BERKLEY BOOKS, NEW YORK

SLOCUM AND THE TRAIL OF DEATH

A Berkley Book / published by arrangement with
the author

PRINTING HISTORY
Berkley edition / July 1991

ISBN: 0-425-12778-8

A Berkley Book ® TM 757,375
Berkley Books are published by The Berkley Publishing Group,
200 Madison Avenue, New York, New York 10016.
The name "BERKLEY" and the "B" logo
are trademarks belonging to Berkley Publishing Corporation.

PRINTED IN THE UNITED STATES OF AMERICA

10 9 8 7 6 5 4 3 2 1

1

It was a land where desperado and drifter, Apache and cut-throat held the promise of sudden death. A sullen sun was hanging low, its rays smoldering on the craggy mountain. Until this moment, it had been a beautiful day for John Slocum.

Seated on the saddle of his roan, he was silent, his lean, powerful body tense, his piercing, green eyes studying the landscape.

He had come on the fresh prints of four riders and two Apaches.

Now the air seemed to breathe with menace; his instinct told him to look and listen. A hawk that had been circling in the golden sky, suddenly plummeted earthward and grabbed a reptile, which squirmed in its claws.

Then the sound of three guns began to sputter, muffled by the nearby cliffs.

Slocum put the roan into a run toward the bulky crags, came off the saddle, gun in hand, and crouching, slipped forward, moving behind rock cover. He peered out.

Two husky, young gunmen had been hiding in ambush and were throwing bullets at a beefy, older man huddled with a young woman behind a big boulder; somehow they had managed to get off their horses and scramble to safety.

Though the man could throw a potshot at the gunmen, they were trapped and it looked bad.

Slocum studied the bushwhackers; they both wore faded shirts, short black hats, spurred boots, and looked plenty mean. One had a moustache. Slocum's teeth gritted; obviously an ambush to rob the man and maybe enjoy the charms of the lady.

The gunmen, concentrating on their quarry, were in clear sight of Slocum's gun. Slocum fired quickly at the nearest bandit, the bullet kicking the Colt from his hand. Startled, the moustachioed gunman swung fast to shoot at the new intruder. Slocum fired again, the bullet tearing into the man's chest, hurling him against the rock; he twisted and fell, his shirt reddening.

The first gunman had grabbed his fist in pain, and was staring in shock at his suddenly dead companion. Aware his own life had been spared, he streaked behind a gathering of rocks where his horse was tethered. Slocum heard the pounding of hooves as the gunman raced north out of sight.

Now the beefy man, who looked like a rancher, came out from behind the boulder, followed by the girl. He was about forty-five, muscled, with a red-skinned, broad-boned face, gray eyes, and a tightly trimmed beard. The young lady wore a pink shirt and tight Levi's; her honey hair glowed under a brown hat. She was peaches and cream, with blue eyes, full lips, and a curvy figure.

They walked to the dead gunman sprawled on the ground and the rancher muttered, "Sonofabitch."

Slocum said nothing. Dead, the gunman didn't look too menacing; he was young, curly haired, with a blond moustache. Slocum hadn't meant to kill, but the dumb kid had forced him. He pulled his shovel, dug a hole, and dropped the bushwhacker in. It was hot and his brow sweated.

When he finished, the beefy hombre came over, put out his hand, and gave Slocum a firm handshake.

"That was the real shootin'. Thank you, mister. I'm James Brogan." He spoke as if expecting immediate recognition.

"Slocum, John Slocum."

"Well, Mr. Slocum, not only did you come in the nick of time, but you did some fancy shootin'." He turned to the young woman. "Ever seen anything like it, honey?" He paused. "My niece, Rosemarie."

Her smile showed even, white teeth; she was a knockout. "No, I haven't. Thank you, Mr. Slocum."

"We been ridin' the trail out of Tucson and ran into these thieving dogs. They almost caught us." Brogan's eyes glittered vindictively as he looked north at the gunman's trail. "One thing I'm sorry about—how come you didn't shoot them *both* dead?" His stare at Slocum was almost accusing.

"I wouldn't have shot *him*, if he hadn't turned his gun on me," Slocum said, jerking his head toward the fresh grave.

"Mr. Slocum is not a bloodthirsty man," Rosemarie said.

Brogan glowered. "They're vicious thieves. Even shootin' was too good for them; they shoulda been strung up."

He pulled out a cigar and lit it. "Slocum, it wouldn't surprise me if that coyote makes another try. I'm carrying precious yellow metal, not much, but a greedy coyote can smell it out. He'll try again." He rubbed his chin thoughtfully. "I'm headed south of Maricopa. Got a ranch there, Silver Fork. It'd be real nice to have a gun like yours along on our trip."

Slocum smiled. "I'd like to help, Mr. Brogan, but I'm going to Phoenix."

Rosemarie's eyes clouded and she looked down; Brogan was astonished. "Listen, Slocum, you bailed us out. There's a hundred in it for you and another hundred when we get there. I've got to get to Maricopa fast." He smiled quickly.

Slocum said nothing.

Brogan's face hardened; he wasn't used to being crossed.

He looked at Rosemarie, then back to Slocum, puffed his cigar, and smiled ruefully. "Fact is, I've got two boys, Gillis and Seth, up there fighting over the ranch. Each wants to squeeze the other out and I'm goin' to settle things. But first I gotta get there." He paused. "And what about Rosemarie? Hate to think what that dirty dog would do if he got hold of this lovely young woman."

Slocum didn't like to think of it either. "What makes you think he'll come at you again?"

"What makes me think it?" Brogan's voice was guttural. "Gold and the girl, that's what. It was a mistake to ride without a couple of my boys." His eyes stared hard into the distance, as if he was trying to see his ranch. "Where you from, if I may ask, Slocum? I hear Southern."

"Georgia."

"I figgered. I'm Texas, myself. We were in the same war, mister. You're a red-blooded Georgia man. We don't want to put Rosemarie at the mercy of a rapin', rotten blue-bellied dog."

Slocum smiled. Brogan was not a man given to modest speech. Then he thought of the Apache tracks he'd seen. Maybe Phoenix could wait.

"I'll mosey along for a time, Mr. Brogan, but if things look quiet for you, I'll go my way."

"You won't regret it." Brogan's gray eyes gleamed viciously as he looked up the trail.

Rosemarie smiled brightly. "Must say, Mr. Slocum, I feel better having you along."

Slocum smiled at her and went for his roan, thinking that Brogan expected trouble on the trail, was sure of it. Slocum wondered why.

• • •

As they rode, the sun slipped lower, singeing the clouds with fiery hues, and painting the peaked mountains with a warm glow.

Finally, they stopped near a rivulet to water the horses, and to rest and drink coffee.

Brogan looked thoughtful as he sipped from his cup; he'd been thinking about the gun attack. "My mind keeps goin' back to those hombres. Can't figger how they knew I had gold."

"Maybe they didn't know," Rosemarie said.

"Oh, they knew." He turned to Slocum. "What do you think?"

"Could be the lady caught their attention," Slocum said.

Brogan rubbed his chest, as if he had an itch; he was thinking hard. "No, I figger they knew somehow."

"Did you get the gold in Tucson?"

"Yup, the bank."

"That could be it. Maybe they picked you up comin' outa the bank. That and a beautiful filly—together, it got their full attention. They followed your trail, then headed you off."

Brogan's gray eyes went jumpy for a moment. He studied Slocum. "You believe the filly's beautiful, mister?"

Slocum tried not to smile. Strange question. She was a knockout, but he sensed that Brogan wasn't crazy about any attention given Rosemarie, even though she was his niece. Some men believed all women, especially the beauties, belonged just to them, like the bull and his herd of cows. Some men were more like bulls than men.

He glanced at Rosemarie—her wide, full lips were wreathed in a smile, like she was amused by Brogan's question, and would be more amused at the answer.

"I reckon most men would find her beautiful," Slocum replied.

Rosemarie's eyes locked on the piercing, green eyes of the stranger. She reached into her pocket for a small kerchief and mopped the thin film of sweat on her upper lip. She was comforted by Slocum's strong presence. When the two gunmen had attacked from behind the cliff, Rosemarie had felt fear. The gunmen had been lurking. Did they know Brogan carried gold? The first shots missed, and Brogan's quick action, racing for the nearby boulder had saved them. Still they'd been trapped and things would have gone bad if not for Slocum. His sharpshooting had done the job. He could have shot both those coyotes dead, but didn't; she liked him for that, although, as Brogan put it, the one might try again. Let a killer get away, he can come back to kill another day.

Brogan was looking at her and she didn't care for his expression. She was beginning to wonder if she'd made a mistake, going to Tucson with him. When they started out, he'd told her he'd take an escort, then changed his mind, believing it might attract attention. Still, these gunmen got on his trail. They weren't drifters, they were gunmen with their eyes on the prize. They were after Brogan's gold and maybe his carcass. They had yelled, "Drop your gun and come out, we may let you live." Did they know him? To her mind, they would have plugged him on the spot. She dreaded to think what would have happened to her then.

That was why she felt this surge of gratitude for Slocum and his sharpshooting.

Brogan was scratching his chin. "I'm thinking those hombres knew we were coming, and they laid for us."

"Well," she said, "I just hope we've seen the last of him."

Slocum looked at the cactus and heavy brush. He remembered the Apache prints, and wondered if he should mention them. It might upset Rosemarie; best to say nothing but keep a doubly sharp lookout.

"So you're from Georgia," she said. "What brings you to this wild country?"

"I shot a man and had to run for it," he said.

She glanced at him. "Who was it?"

"He was a judge," Slocum said dryly. "He had a piece of paper that said he'd come into possession of our plantation, the land that belonged to the Slocums for generations. He was a carpetbagger. I gave him a bullet instead of the land. That's when I decided it might be a good idea to go west."

Rosemarie smiled. She liked the green-eyed Slocum, the calm, confident look of him, his strong face, his powerful body.

It would be nice to have him along on the trail ahead.

2

They started to ride, and Brogan, in a hurry, pushed his sorrel out front.

Slocum caught up. "Best not to ride that fast."

Brogan scowled. "I'm in a hurry, Slocum. Got a long way to go and things to do."

"Folks in a hurry reach a quick grave," Slocum said.

Brogan's jaw tightened and he pulled up. "What the hell's that mean?"

Slocum gazed at the dense brush and thick foliage lining the trail, good sites for ambush.

"It pays to look at the tracks," he said.

Brogan shrugged. "What the hell, that gunslinger is nothin' to worry 'bout. You said it yourself. He's got no gun, wouldn't come at us again."

"It's not the gunslinger I'm thinkin' of. It's the Apache."

Brogan jerked his head around to stare.

"I've been keeping a sharp lookout," Slocum said. "I was hopin' they'd go west when we hit the river, but they didn't. They're out in front on this trail. We'll move carefully."

Brogan threw a nervous glance at Rosemarie. "Whyn't you tell us about the Apaches, mister?"

Slocum shrugged. "Didn't want to worry you. But they didn't go west at the river."

Brogan looked thoughtful. "Might be coincidence, them travelin' our trail."

"Might not."

"All right—we'll slow down," Brogan said.

Slocum took the lead and whenever they reached a site that lent itself to ambush, Slocum would study it, then move carefully.

They traveled for another hour through a heavy spread of brush until Slocum abruptly held up his hand. He had caught the glint of metal in the sun. He listened, looked, his face hardening.

"What is it?" Brogan's voice grated; he hated this forced slowdown for two drifting Apaches, but had to recognize that caution was the better part of valor.

He watched Slocum move the roan ahead carefully, gun in hand, pausing to listen.

Then Slocum turned, grim-faced. "Wait here."

He found the gunslinger lying on his back, a bloody mess. He'd been scalped and his neck showed a thick, gaping, bloody gash. His horse was gone and he'd been stripped of his boots and shirt.

Slocum came forward, jaw set hard. He had ruined the hombre's gun, and the poor bastard had the bad luck to cross the path of two vicious Apaches.

"Those murderin' Apache dogs," Brogan growled.

Slocum stared at him; he had brought Rosemarie. "I told you to wait."

Brogan gritted his teeth, then glanced quickly at a clump of brush, as if he, too, could be a target. "Let's get the hell outa here," he said.

"I'll bury him."

Brogan didn't like it. "How d'ya know they're not watching us, waitin' for an opening?"

Slocum shrugged. "I looked at the tracks."

"It's a waste of time. We need to move fast."

"Won't take long. Can't leave him, don't want the buzzards to get at him, too." Slocum looked at the body. "Feel sorta responsible. He had no chance without a gun."

Brogan scowled. "What the hell—you feelin' sorry for him? He was a thieving coyote."

Slocum's voice was cold. "Mister, nobody deserves to die like that."

He pulled his shovel and dug the grave while they watched. After dropping the bandit in the hole, he mumbled a prayer. The words didn't come clear to Rosemarie. "What'd you say?" she asked.

He smiled. "God works in mysterious ways."

"Meaning?" she asked.

"God saved him from my gun but gave him to the Apache tomahawks."

Brogan grimaced. "Got the kinda death he deserved." He turned to the horses. "Now, let's start."

"No, not yet," Slocum said.

They looked at him.

"I'm goin' after the Apaches," he said.

"Are you crazy?" Brogan scowled. "We don't have time for that. I told you over and over, I'm in a hurry to get back."

"Yes, but you're not goin' to get back unless we do something about the Apaches."

Brogan's face was reddening. "Listen, we don't bother them, they won't bother us."

"Like they didn't bother the gunslinger?" Slocum paused and lit a cigarillo. "They know we're here, and if we don't take them, they'll take us. Best to pick the time and place rather than wait for them to do it."

Rosemarie looked at him. "What do we do?"

"Stay on the trail; just ride behind me. I'll move up front.

And don't worry about me, I'll pick you up before sundown."

Slocum stayed alert on the trail, his green eyes sharply studying boulders, ravines, dense brush, whatever held the threat of ambush. Danger lurked and he knew if he lost his concentration he wouldn't survive.

Slocum followed the fresh tracks. There were, he knew, Apaches who were always in a rage, who ruthlessly hunted the intruding paleface who had invaded his land and violated his people. Born to warfare, the Apache could read signs and move with the craft of the fox. Slocum in his time had fought Comanche and Sioux, but the Apache was the toughest of all. Judging from their work on the gunman, the two he trailed were vicious.

When he came to a small stream, he stopped to study the other side; it looked clear. He crossed the stream and noted to his surprise the emerging tracks of only *one* horse. Slocum's jaw hardened: the tracks out of the stream showed a quickened pace to reach the thick brush ahead. Slocum believed they had expected him and separated, one riding downstream, the other ahead. What were they after? To circle him or did they have something else in mind? This diversion spelled danger; Slocum tensed as he tried to get into the Apache mind. The trail ahead moved into heavy growth. Not bad for ambush, but Slocum ignored it; the danger came from the Apache who was trying to conceal his trail by riding the stream. Would he go down or up? It depended on what he wanted. And Slocum suddenly knew what he wanted.

Instead of riding in the water, Slocum recrossed it and rode until he saw the fresh unshod tracks—a circling movement, as he had figured. A quiver went through him. He kicked at the roan, and the horse, recognizing the urgency, put his ears back and began to race, his hooves pounding the earth.

Slocum had his gun out when he reached Brogan, leaning against a rock, pulling at an arrow in his shoulder, his face wrenched with pain. The girl was gone.

"He came outa nowhere," Brogan growled. "He's got my gun, and he's got her. That way," he pointed.

It took only minutes for Slocum to pick up sound in a patch circled by rocks and brush. Silently he crept forward, until through the brush he could glimpse the Apache, big-chested, muscular, Brogan's gun in hand. He was leaning over Rosemarie, sprawled on the ground, staring up. The Apache reached out his hand to her shirt and sudden-ly froze, then with amazing quickness, fired in Slocum's direction. The bullet whistled past him, forcing him to roll on the ground; the Apache grabbed Rosemarie as if she was featherlight and held her in front of him, as a shield. Then to Slocum's astonishment, this bold dog, instead of retreating for cover, came directly toward him. A fiendish trick that froze Slocum's gun; the redskin was using the squaw, aware the paleface enemy would not fire.

When the Apache raised his gun, Slocum ducked for cover behind a half-buried rock; the Apache's bullet kicked close at the dirt.

Slocum's nerves tingled; he felt helpless, he was a target yet couldn't shoot back, he was in a bad position and could easily hit Rosemarie. The Apache fired again, this time the bullet splintered the rock. He stepped forward slowly, his dark face grinning because he had the paleface in a death trap. Slocum felt desperate and wondered if he should chance a shot. Then Rosemarie, using all her strength, sud-denly twisted her body, her fingers clawing at the Apache's eyes. He jerked his head back and Slocum's move was lightning-quick as he fired his gun, the bullet smashing the Apache's head, shearing off part of his skull. He reeled back, eyes glazed, legs collapsing, and dropped Rosemarie. She lifted herself, glanced coldly at the sprawled Indian, then ran to Slocum. Her face was flushed; she grabbed his face in her hands and kissed him.

Slocum grinned, then walked to the dead Indian, took Brogan's gun, and stuck it in his gunbelt.

3

When they reached Brogan, he had tugged out the arrow. A little bleeding, but it didn't seem to bother him, he was wrapping the wound in cloth. He looked relieved to see Rosemarie apparently unhurt.

"Hope you hit that redskin where he should be hit," he growled. "You all right, Rosemarie?"

She nodded brightly. "Slocum has a habit of turning up at the right moment." She looked at him solicitously. "What about you, James? Is it bad?"

"That Apache dogface was too excited at the sight of you to shoot straight. Just nicked my shoulder." He bit his lip. "I figgered you were a goner after that big bastard got holt of you."

"It almost happened," she said.

Brogan glared at Slocum. "What the hell took you so long? Thought you were trackin' them."

Slocum's eyes narrowed. "That's what brought me back here."

Brogan's voice grated. "Well, if you got here faster, I wouldn't have had to pull an arrow outa my flesh."

Rosemarie frowned. "Slocum did the job when he *did* come, you want to keep that in mind, James."

"That's what a gunfighter gets paid for, Rosemarie."

She flushed. "I escaped by the skin of my teeth, and you can believe that after the Apache got through with me, he'd come back to finish you. Maybe we owe Mr. Slocum some thanks."

Slocum scowled, thinking that Brogan was a bit of a buzzard, and it'd be nice to drop him cold. But there was another Apache out there, and he didn't like to leave Rosemarie in a spot. He said nothing.

Brogan glanced at Slocum and read his anger, but he didn't care. He thought of Slocum as a hired gunfighter—there to do his job. But he'd been outwitted by the Apache, which got him the arrow, and put Rosemarie at risk for violence. Brogan thought that his top gun at Silver Fork, Dick Mire, would have done better. But nothing had happened to Rosemarie, that was the main thing. He thought of Seth back at the ranch—that boy would have gone hog-wild if the Apache had got to Rosemarie.

"The Apache used me as a body shield, while he kept shooting at Slocum," Rosemarie added.

"What did Slocum do?" Brogan demanded quickly.

"He didn't fire, not 'til I scratched the Apache's eyes. Only then did he use his gun."

"Glad you thought of that, miss," Slocum said. "His next bullet would have done it."

Brogan cleared his throat. He didn't like Slocum's heroics, didn't like Rosemarie admiring him. "Well," he said grumpily. "All's well that ends well. We've got plenty of riding ahead, so let's git."

"There's another Apache out there," Slocum said.

Brogan grimaced. "One redskin ain't gonna do much damage. He'll probably ride on."

"We don't know that," Slocum said. "Might want revenge for his comrade."

Brogan shook his head. "We don't know that, either. The town of Redstone ain't too far, so let's ride."

Slocum watched the land as the sun started down in a sky glowing with gold, and the great shoulders of raw, red rock caught the light. He kept a sharp eye out for the Apache, but found no trace. When they reached Redstone it was evening, and the air had cooled. The main street was broad, dusty, and busy; the houses on either side were weather-beaten.

As they walked their horses down the street, Brogan out front, Slocum noted two cowboys sitting on tilted chairs on the hotel porch; one of them, stalwart and red-faced, was staring hard at Brogan. Slocum couldn't help wonder what that cowboy had in mind.

Brogan paid no attention, he was headed for the saloon, eager to get there. Probably thirst, but there was something odd about him, Slocum thought. On the surface he seemed okay, somewhat crusty, not exactly bighearted—a rich rancher, with two sons who were slugging it out for the ranch. But what the hell was all that about gold? And about Rosemarie: she never called him uncle. And Brogan's attitude was strange, he seemed jealous. Helluva uncle. And he was in a sweat to get back to Silver Fork ranch. Had a lot on his mind, didn't he?

Slocum shrugged. If not for the beautiful Rosemarie, he'd drop Brogan in a minute. He sighed; wouldn't mind a coupla snorts himself at the saloon.

They put the horses in the livery barn, and dropped Rosemarie at the hotel; she could use the rest.

Then they strolled to Riley's two-story saloon.

It was a big saloon with a long bar, plenty of customers, a few ladies in bright dresses, tables for card players, and rooms upstairs for play of a different kind.

They went to the bar.

"Whiskey, Riley, you got a coupla thirsty men," Brogan said.

"Yes, sir, Mr. Brogan." He slapped two glasses on the bar and filled them.

Brogan gulped his drink and the barman refilled it. "Damn, that whiskey's a bit raw." But Brogan polished off the second drink, too, and wiped his lips.

"Best I can get these days," Riley said. He noticed the bandage. "Run into trouble, Mr. Brogan?"

"A bit. Couple of Apaches. I caught an arrow, but we finished him. This here is Slocum. Not a bad shooter."

Slocum smiled. Brogan's enthusiasm for his shooting had lessened since he had caught the arrow.

Brogan was looking at the card players. "Figger on spending the night at the hotel, Slocum. Rosemarie needs the rest, and I'm saddle sore. Mebbe we'll play a bit o' poker and pick up some extra money from these dumb coyotes."

The whiskey did have a harsh bite, but Slocum didn't mind. He drank another and looked around the saloon, especially at the ladies . A buxom wench caught his eye; lots of flesh packed in the right places. He figured it would be nice to spear that one to a mattress.

Softened by his third drink, Brogan turned to Slocum, and spoke in a friendly voice. "Maybe I was a bit sharp on the trail. Got a lot on my mind."

Slocum nodded, wondering if Brogan had some grace in him, after all, but for the moment, he was caught up looking at the buxom wench. She had blond hair, a big bust, a small waist, and a pretty face with full lips and widely-spaced eyes.

"It's the ranch," Brogan said. "The way my boys are squabbling over it, I figger something bad might happen. It's on my mind." Brogan poured another drink. "These boys of mine, Gillis and Seth, are headstrong. Don't get along. Something bad could happen, blood could spill. I have to get there. It's me that's got to stop it."

Brogan's gray eyes stared at Slocum, then they went blank and he looked away.

Slocum reached for his drink. You couldn't tell about Brogan; he talked straight, but somehow seemed slippery. And you had to wonder how Brogan brought up his kids, to make them hack at each other, to believe land more important than kinship. Maybe Brogan got the kids he deserved— the seed didn't fall far from the tree.

"I especially worry about Seth, a hothead, you can't trust a boy like him," Brogan said.

The batwing doors swung open and two cowboys swaggered in. Slocum recognized the curly haired, red-cheeked, hefty hombre who had stared at Brogan from the hotel porch. This time his glance at Brogan was casual as he strolled to the card tables, followed by his sidekick. From there he glanced again at Brogan, his mouth grim. Something about Brogan seemed to fascinate the hombre.

Now Slocum's eyes strayed to the buxom wench who elected to sit alone, nursing a drink. He had never seen such an appetizing dish in a saloon. His eyes caressed the pink flesh of her bosom, plenty of which showed in her low-cut dress. Slocum felt tingles in his groin.

Just then an unkempt, stubble-bearded cowboy staggered in front of her, leaned down with a leer and whispered in her ear. She fixed him with an icy stare and flung her drink in his face. Then she stood up, silently facing him.

The saloon was suddenly silent, watching the drunk. He reached slowly into his pocket, pulled out a mottled, red kerchief, wiped his face, glared at her with his red, boozy eyes, looked around, then said loudly, "That's one helluva waste of whiskey, Tina."

Men laughed, and one cowboy yelled, "You're messin' with a dangerous gal, Luke." The men went back to what they were doing.

Tina didn't smile, she just strolled to the bar, and Slocum watched her. Some women put you in mind of the bed by just moving.

She must have picked up something from him, for she stopped suddenly, her gray-blue eyes locked on his. Her lips curved and she stopped in front of him.

He smiled. "I'd offer you a drink, Tina, if I could be sure you wouldn't throw it at me."

Tina's face wreathed in a smile. "It's not the sort of thing I'd throw at you." She jerked her thumb at the drunk. "Some critters don't know how to talk to a lady."

Then, glancing at Brogan, her eyes chilled as if she didn't like what she saw. Turning back to Slocum, she asked, "Been riding hard, cowboy?"

Hard riding, he thought; Tina picked her words with care.

She went on. "Maybe you won't mind a bit of relaxing."

"You're reading my mind," Slocum said.

Her full lips broadened in a lazy, sensual smile. "Come up to the last room on the left when you feel like it. You'll find me there." As she walked up the stairs, Slocum watched the movement of her buttocks—pure poetry.

"What the hell do you want to waste time with that for, Slocum?"

Slocum gave Brogan a cool stare. "Maybe you're a little tired to be interested in the ladies. Not me."

Brogan scowled. "Don't like saloon women."

"For a traveling man like me, such ladies are a great comfort."

Brogan shook his head. "Maybe you oughta strike root and find a decent woman, Slocum."

"Like Rosemarie, maybe?"

Brogan's jaw hardened; he didn't like the idea at all. In fact, the idea seemed to offend him. "Slocum, I didn't have Rosemarie in mind."

Slocum rubbed his chin. This hombre really had an attitude about his niece. Maybe he figured that filly belonged to one of his sons, and the idea made him churn that anyone else would put his hands on her lily-white body.

He was ready to tell Brogan he had had enough of his sour company, and he could ride to Silver Fork on his own, but he thought of Rosemarie, and things that could happen on the trail.

"Well, whoever gets Rosemarie gets a real peach," Slocum said, and turned to look at the gamblers.

After awhile he eyed the balcony. "Reckon I'll go up those stairs. Like the lady says, a man needs a bit of relaxing after a day of hard riding."

"Okay, I'll be here. Maybe I'll mosey over to the card games."

For a moment Slocum thought of suggesting that he keep an eye on the red-cheeked hombre, now sitting in the game, but shrugged it off. There could be plenty of reasons for one man to stare at another.

He walked through the smoky, noisy saloon to the stairs, passing the drunk, Luke, who was watching him. A bit on the loco side, Slocum thought; Luke had seen Tina talk to him and he didn't know what went through his whiskey-soaked brain.

When he opened the last door upstairs, the sight of Tina sitting on a chair holding a glass was a delightful shock. She was almost nude, except for a skimpy, silk chemise and all the promise of her buxom beauty that he'd seen downstairs was now joltingly visible. Full breasts, not oversized, but in proportion to the ample flesh of her body. Silky flesh, pink nipples, abundant hips, and well-formed legs; he could see the blond hair peeping between her thighs. For a saloon lady, she was special.

"Well," she said, her voice just a touch slurred, "'bout time you made it. To tell the truth I've been achin' for you to come up. You look like a man who'd be mighty interestin' to a woman."

He grinned. "And you look like a woman who could inspire a man to do his best. Slocum's the name."

She pointed to the bottle on the table. "Do my glass, Slocum. And tell me why a man like you is travelin' with a man like him."

"Him? You mean Brogan?"

"Yeah. He didn't like me much, did he?"

"I wouldn't say that."

"Don't hafta. I read it in his face. A mean hombre. Watch out for him."

"What d'ya mean?" He gave her the glass.

She sipped the whiskey. "He's a man who talks with a forked tongue."

Slocum had to laugh. "You can't tell a thing like that from two minutes with a man. A man could talk with a forked tongue and have a big heart."

"You think he's got a big heart?" She looked doubtful.

"He gave his big ranch to his two kids. Sounds generous."

"He did? Surprises me. I wouldn't trust him with a tin dime."

Slocum scowled. He was a bit baffled by Brogan himself, but it seemed more his attitude than anything he did.

To hell with it, he'd be through with Brogan when they got to Maricopa, he had committed himself, in a way, to take him there. Was it the money or Rosemarie? The thought of her brought his mind back to Tina. Rosemarie was a girl he might yearn for, but seemed beyond his reach. Tina was here, in the flesh, ready and willing. A bird in hand . . .

She stared at him. "Why do you still have your clothes on, Slocum?"

"'Cause you're talking up a storm, that's why."

It took him moments to strip.

She smiled. "You been standin' there, all this time, with that upstanding thing?"

"It's been like that since I saw you downstairs," he said, straight-faced.

"You poor man. Come closer, see if I can be of some help."

He grinned and came toward her. She leaned into him and did some mighty impressive things with great skill. After a time, he pulled her to her feet and began to stroke her body, her rounded buttocks, her slender waist. His hands moved over her full breasts, her slightly rounded belly. His tongue flicked at her nipples, his finger moved between her thighs. Her body responded, she was one passionate lady.

He brought her to the bed where she lay back, eyes glittering. He straddled her and slipped into the snug, wet warmth. He began to move with strong rhythm, his hands behind her silky buttocks, pausing at times to caress her body, then resuming his drive. Suddenly she grabbed him, stiffening as her body pulsated. He prolonged his pleasure until the tension became too intense, then he drove powerfully until he hit the peak. She screamed softly.

Slocum had just stepped into his long johns when the door quietly opened, and there stood Luke, his boozy, red eyes glaring at Tina—he held a gun in his hand.

"You slut. Did you think I was goin' to let you get away with what you did to me down there? Shamin' me in front of all them folks."

"Luke," she said, "You aimin' to shoot a woman?"

"Goin' to put a bullet up your tail—and throw this feller

in free. No witnesses." He grinned fiercely.

Slocum's gun was in its holster on the chair. He smiled. "Hey, Luke. I don't blame you. A woman throwing booze in my face—I'd pay her off, too."

"I'm not talkin' to you, cowboy. You got no beef. You're goin' out after a good screw."

"Wait a minute, Luke. How you going to get away with it? They'll string you up."

Luke grinned. "Naw. I'm goin' to shoot her with your gun. Shoot you, then put the gun in your hand, like you shot her, then did yourself." He showed his yellow teeth. "Yuh couldn't stand the pleasure. Not bad, hey cowboy?"

Slocum nodded admiringly—for a drunk, the sonofabitch had imagination. He waited as Luke turned to the holster on the chair to pull out the gun, then Slocum flung the pillow at the critter's face, confusing him for the second he needed. He grabbed Luke's gun wrist with his powerful hands, jerked, and pulled him to the window, sending Luke crashing through it. He plunged headfirst two stories and hit the ground with a thud. He lay there, with a broken neck, still clutching his gun.

Slocum stared down at him for a moment. "A little more excitement than I expected in this room," he muttered as he swiftly slipped into his Levi's.

"What happened out there?" Tina asked.

Slocum paused at the door. "I think we've seen the last of Luke."

Downstairs, he walked to the bar, motioned to Riley, and spoke softly. "We had a rumpus upstairs, and Luke took a flying leap through your window. He's lying outside, with a permanent crick in his neck. Better send for your burying man."

Riley stared, then turned to a bearded man drinking at the

bar. He whispered in his ear; the man nodded, and went out the door. Riley came back to Slocum and smiled. "I'm surprised that Luke lasted as long as he did. Born to have a short, nasty life."

"Reckon," drawled Slocum, glancing around the saloon. Brogan was playing in the poker game with the red-cheeked hombre. Slocum sauntered over.

Brogan had lots of chips in front of him, and the hombre was losing. This seemed to give Brogan plenty of pleasure. Slocum watched Brogan top the hombre's jacks with a pair of queens.

As Brogan raked in the pot, he said, "Hey, Berne, didn't you say you'd teach me the fine art of poker?" His gray eyes gleamed with amusement. "I'm still waiting for the lesson."

The dealer had dealt a new hand, and Berne picked up his cards, his broad face twisting in a grimace. "One thing, mister, you can't beat in life is Lady Luck. Trouble is, the Lady is a whore; don't care *who* she favors."

Brogan's eyes were icy. "Berne, you talk like you play poker—lousy."

Berne looked at his cards, then dropped them on the table. He glanced at Slocum, as if measuring him in case of trouble, then turned to Brogan.

"I'm just thinkin' of your name, mister. I heard of a Brogan once, but it couldn't be you. This was a big rancher near Maricopa."

"I got a ranch there," Brogan said.

"You do?" Berne studied Brogan with a hard jaw. "But it couldn't be you. This hombre, I heard, was a rustlin', rotten coyote. Had a bunch of gunfighters, and one of them shot my brother, Rafe. I didn't learn about it 'til later."

Brogan looked around the table, then said, "What the hell's all that about, mister? What'd you say the rustler's name was?"

"Brogan, James Brogan."

"What the hell's this, some kinda joke?" Brogan asked fiercely.

"Why say that?"

"That's my name. No Brogan I know ever did any rustlin'. I'da strung him up myself. I got a ranch with more than a thousand steers."

There was a long pause while Berne stared at Brogan. His sidekick, a dark, sinewy cowboy, moved closer to Berne.

Slocum studied the glint in Berne's brown eyes and stiffened.

"Well, Brogan," said Berne, rising to his feet, "I'm goin' to shoot you to kingdom come."

The men nearby scrambled to the side of the saloon.

Slocum spoke up, aware that Brogan, an older man, didn't have the reflexes to match this loco. "Hold it," he said. "You've got no quarrel with Mr. Brogan. It's the wrong man."

"Stay outa this," Berne hissed, "if you want to keep your skin whole."

Slocum kept his voice measured. "Listen, mister, I've got no beef against you, but I'm not going to let you showdown with Mr. Brogan."

Berne grinned viciously. "I'm goin' to send *Mister* Brogan to hell, and if you want to make the trip with him, it's your funeral."

Everyone in the saloon watched, fascinated.

Moving into a gun crouch, Berne hissed at Slocum. "Your last chance, mister, step aside, you can live."

"It's you who has to step aside," Slocum said.

"I'll teach you to horn in," Berne growled, and he went for his gun. He was fast, much faster than Slocum expected. He had his gun out of the holster and on the rise when Slocum's

.44 bullet hit; it hurled him back over his chair and he fell hard to the floor and lay there.

His sidekick, with an incredulous stare at Slocum, rushed to the bleeding man, who had been hit in his right shoulder, not a mortal wound.

"Somebody get Dr. Wilson," he yelled.

Slocum tugged at Brogan, who had been stupefied by the quick action, and nudged him to the door.

Out in the street, Brogan looked at Slocum in amazement. "That hombre was loco. Where'd he get that crazy nonsense?"

"Maybe he was out to get you, Brogan, from the moment he saw you."

"What's that mean?"

"When we rode into town, he was looking at you mean-eyed from the hotel porch. I didn't think too much about it then, but he had you on his kill list, for some reason."

Brogan looked back at the saloon. "Let's get the hell outa this town. It stinks. We'll pick up Rosemarie and sleep on the trail."

4

Rosemarie wasn't crazy about the change of plan, hoping to sleep the night in a comfortable hotel bed, but she didn't complain.

For a couple of hours they rode in the dusk, until Slocum spotted good cover with thick brush and boulders.

They made a fire in a pit and settled down while Brogan smoked a cigar. Slocum sipped coffee and watched the moon rise on the horizon, silvering the vast crags in the distance.

Brogan turned to Slocum. "So you figgered that polecat had me on target?"

Slocum said nothing.

"If you believed it, why didn't you shoot to kill? You seem able to put a bullet where you want."

"I mighta been wrong."

Brogan's brow wrinkled with thought. "Mebbe it was the gold. Looks like the polecat got a tip-off that I'd be carrying gold. They're out to mow me down."

Slocum rubbed his chin. "Might be. Somebody's after your hide. Gotta be a reason."

Rosemarie looked thoughtful. "What reason, I wonder?"

In the silence, a coyote howled mournfully at the moon.

Another in the distance echoed the doleful howl.

Slocum smiled at the sound and looked at the moon spilling silver over the bushy landscape. He became thoughtful. "Might there be another reason for him to target you?" Glancing at Brogan, he was surprised by his tight face.

"Maybe you've got some idea?" Slocum persisted.

That jarred Brogan and he shot Slocum a suspicious look, as if resenting Slocum trying to read his mind. "No," he said scowling. "Can't think of another reason."

"Let's hope we're through with them now," Rosemarie said.

"They keep coming outa the woodwork," Slocum said.

"But they go into the ground." Brogan grinned. "Thanks to your fast gun, Slocum. That polecat was a gunfighter. I couldn't handle him. You keep saving my skin. I'll show my thanks when we get to the Silver Fork."

"It's good having Slocum with us," Rosemarie said, smiling at him.

Slocum gazed with pleasure at her peaches-and-cream face, the full, kissing lips, and cornflower-blue eyes.

Brogan's mood suddenly changed. "Well, we've got a lot of ridin' tomorrow, best we get some shut-eye now."

Slocum dreamed.

He heard the coyote in his sleep; in the dark it ran along the edge of his mind, he dreamed the coyote had grabbed a rabbit in its sharp jaws and was running hard; he was tracking it. The coyote suddenly stopped, dropped the rabbit, turned, and showed vicious fangs, its yellow eyes glittering with evil light. It jarred Slocum, and he was aware that he didn't have his gun. He drew his knife. Then, to his amazement, the coyote turned into an Apache who threw his tomahawk, which struck Slocum on the side of the head.

He groaned in his sleep, awakening, and became aware he lay heavy against the side of his head. He listened to the sounds, the night hawk, the coyote's howl, the slithering of something through brush. His eyes snapped open.

The moon still silvered the land; Slocum's glance moved to Brogan, snoring softly in his bedroll nearby. Quickly his gaze shifted to Rosemarie's bedroll, on the other side of their camp.

Empty!

His hand stole to his gun as he lifted his head slightly for a better view. She was gone, nowhere in sight. Slocum felt a quiver, wondering if what he feared two days ago had happened now. He got up softly, moved closer to where she had slept and saw the moccasin print. He followed the tracks for a few moments then quickly came back to Brogan and touched his shoulder.

Brogan stirred sleepily, opened his eyes, looked at Slocum, and was about to complain, but something stopped him cold. With shiny, anxious eyes, he sat up. Instinctively, he turned to where Rosemarie had slept. It jerked him to his feet.

"It's the Apache," Slocum said.

Brogan turned pale. "He's got Rosemarie?"

Slocum nodded, and went back to the prints. The Apache had come in silently and decided to grab the greater prize, the girl. That would partly revenge the death of his comrade. He smothered her, preventing her from screaming, maybe conked her, and carried her off to his horse.

Slocum's jaw tightened; that might be a mistake, riding a double burden would slow him down.

"Dammit, Slocum. How'd we sleep through that?"

"He's an Apache," Slocum said. "Quiet, patient. He trailed us, waited for us to ride through town. Revenge for his comrade."

Brogan thought a moment, then looked guilty. "Reckon you were right. I should have let you go after him back there."

It was what Slocum had been thinking. Now the Apache had Rosemarie, he was twice as dangerous, he could hurt her, do worse.

"Stay here," Slocum said. "I'll trail him. It's faster. His tracks are fresh, he can't be that far. If I'm not back in three hours, well, do what you have to."

He slipped into the roan's saddle and followed the moccasin tracks; they were heavy, he was carrying the girl. About one hundred yards away there were tracks of the Apache's horse. Fresh tracks.

It was daybreak at the horizon, the dark was draining out of the sky. Slocum looked grim as he remembered his dream of the coyote with the rabbit in his mouth.

What would a revenging Apache do? Was he using Rosemarie as bait to trap the paleface? He might take her with force, even kill her—that would hurt the paleface he knew would track him. Or he could abuse her, then leave the leftover for the paleface to mourn. After he had given the paleface such pain, he would then try to capture, torture, and kill.

These thoughts slipped through Slocum's mind as he stayed on the tracks. He had been gaining, the track looked fresher. A half hour later, Slocum saw the kind of land that the Apache might use to work out his designs. A rise with thickets, dense brush, plenty of rocks. Perfect for ambush, and for violence against Rosemarie.

Slocum studied the land: the Apache didn't hide his tracks, he had nothing to fear.

Slocum thought of the moves he must make, going up the slope. . . .

● ● ●

From dense brush, on the top of the slope, the Apache had seen Slocum dart quickly behind a boulder and look up. The Apache was powerful, thick-muscled, with a brown, broad face and dark eyes that gleamed with hate. He had recognized the paleface below, the lean, strong one who did not look easy. The Apache knew from the signs this one had killed Red Fox.

This paleface dog was coming: the one he wanted. He must die, and die in pain. The Apache thought of his own pain, his blood brother, Red Fox, dead, their land despoiled, their women and children hunted like animals. The Apache's hate was justified. He had tracked the three palefaces to the town, and waited for them to pass through, going north.

It had cost time, but the Apache knew about patience. And he knew about the paleface squaw, a beauty. He knew what to do, to grab her in the night which would bring the lean warrior to him.

The Apache smiled grimly. The white man could not stand for his woman to be taken: that was the worst insult. The Apache looked down at the squaw. She lay silent, breathing slowly; he had given her a hard blow. He had tied her hands, gagged her; now she watched him through slitted eyes. A beautiful paleface—he would have taken her if there had been time.

But the big warrior had come quicker than expected. It did not matter. He would enjoy the squaw after he killed this paleface. Then he'd hunt the older one, slit his throat. They had to pay for the death of Red Fox. Each paleface who died, made the hurt easier in the Apache's heart.

He waited, and knew what to do.

Slocum crouched behind the boulder, aware that time was on the side of the Apache. The sun creeping up would make his visibility better. And he'd be sitting up there, on top of that rise, waiting. He had to be there, the tracks were fresh.

Slocum pondered: did the Apache have a rifle? The Apache that he had killed had no rifle, just the gun taken from Brogan. A good chance this one wouldn't have a rifle, either, he'd have a knife, a tomahawk, and the incredible war skills of his tribe.

Still, he had to test for the rifle—he put his hat on the barrel of his gun, an old trick, and raised it slowly, slightly. He held it there.

Nothing.

He raised the hat further. Still nothing.

He had to climb that slope. He studied the terrain, the cover that he must use, different rocks, clumps of brush, tree stumps, these could bring him close to the top. But every move had to be right.

Just because the Apache didn't shoot did not mean he had no rifle, he might be playing a game. He was an Apache burning with revenge, and what could be more fearsome. He might want to capture his enemy alive and do some harsh tricks. You didn't get second chances when you fought the Apache.

Gun in hand, Slocum took his time going up, moving with catlike steps from one cover to the next, and when he moved, he never took his eyes off the crest of the slope, just in case the Apache showed his head.

He moved so slowly that by the time he got to within fifteen feet of the crest, the rays of the rising sun were tinting the clouds with pink fire.

Now Slocum felt the muscles in his gut knotted by the suspense. Could he be wrong about the Apache? Perhaps he did not stop after all. But he would bypass this position only if he had something better in mind. Was he double-tracking?

No, the tracks were fresh. He had to be there, just over the crest, with Rosemarie. Maybe without a rifle, but he had the knife.

Slocum, his body wet with sweat, his muscles aching with the strain, his clothes smeared with dirt, huddled behind his last boulder, and tried to get into the Apache's mind. He was there, he was waiting, and he would attack the moment Slocum came over the rise. What worried Slocum most was Rosemarie's silence. What had the Apache done to her? The thought pierced him, and the anger energized him after his long, laborious climb.

He figured his last move: he could rush over the top, gun ready to shoot, but he'd be a target standing upright. Or he could crawl over, stay low, and be ready to shoot instantly.

He elected to go over crouched, at an angle; to do the unexpected was the best warfare.

He took a deep breath, and moving quick and catlike, he went over, his finger on the trigger, his body mobilized, his eyes raking the scene.

No Apache! Anywhere.

But Rosemarie was there, lying prone, hands tied, a gag in her mouth.

Not dead? Had he hurt her and left her—his revenge?

Slocum's instinct was to rush over, but he didn't move. The Apache was the most cunning of warriors; something was happening—what?

Slocum took several steps, then suddenly stopped. His nerves shrieking, he wheeled around and there was the Apache, right behind him, knife in hand, a big, muscled body, a bullet head, and eyes glittering with fury, with triumph. He had brought the paleface into his trap, used the girl as bait, and he had come out of the ground.

The Apache had wanted the paleface to know, to kill him

slowly, but this one had been too quick. He struck viciously at the gun hand, and the gun dropped.

The Apache brought his knife down to stab, but Slocum caught his thick wrist with his own powerful hand, and they stood like that, like statues, legs planted to the ground, straining nerve and muscle, one to stab and kill, the other to stop him.

Rosemarie's eyes glittered as she watched the death struggle, but she couldn't move; she watched them as if in a trance.

They strained against each other with all their might, their muscles standing out like cords, each aware the loser would pay with his life. Slocum was staring into the strange, brown eyes and he could see the depths of hell. Finally, summoning every ounce of his strength, Slocum wrenched the Apache's wrist and heard the crack of bone. The knife dropped to the ground. Instantly the Apache's left hand darted to claw Slocum's throat. But Slocum, using both hands, pulled the hand away, and butted the Apache, who fell to the ground. Lightning quick, Slocum grabbed the knife as the Apache sprung up, rushing forward only to catch the full thrust of the knife in his chest.

The Apache grunted, stumbled, fell, and lay there, realizing his defeat. A terrible look of sorrow slowly appeared in his eyes: he felt he had failed his comrade, failed his tribe, and would die without revenge.

He lay back, breathing hard, his gaze riveted to the pale face. And dying, the Apache could not help but feel wonder at this paleface who somehow had bested him.

He closed his eyes and died.

Slocum, too, looked sorrowful. The Apache lay in dignity, a valiant foe who fought for what he believed in, loyalty to his friend, and his people, and for survival. There was nobility in such death.

• • •

Slocum unloosed the thongs that bound Rosemarie's hands and took the gag from her mouth. Her eyes were blazing; her feelings had been rioting as she witnessed the fight. Horror, when the Apache's knife seemed about to annihilate Slocum; terror, as they wrestled for mastery, and as the fight went on, awareness that her destiny was involved with Slocum.

The sudden death of the Apache triggered feelings too great for her to control. Instead of violation she had been saved. When Slocum unleashed her hands, she grabbed him, holding his face, kissing him full on the lips, pressing hard against him, as if she wanted her body to pass into him.

And Slocum, still taut from the battle, felt the primal urges that come to a man after he's destroyed his enemy, and felt the exultation of surviving the threat of death. Nothing seemed more natural than to embrace the woman, the prize after combat. Their instincts connected. It took less than a minute before they were naked and tight against each other, and she had drawn his excitement into her flesh.

Slocum was feverishly aware of her beautiful body, its marvelous curve of hip, her full, firm breasts, her silky skin, the delight of her secret, inner warmth. But there was no crafty coupling, it was all instinctive, natural, swift, and in its climax, ecstatic—a release from the terrible tension spawned by the threat of death and the joy of survival.

After laying silently together, they came back to themselves.

Nothing was said.

Then Slocum pulled out a cigarillo and lit it. "It's no small thing when a warrior like that dies," he mused.

She looked at him curiously, but said nothing.

He buried the Apache.

When he came back to her, she looked more herself.

"If you hadn't come," she said, "I would have been dead by now. Either the Apache would have done it, or I would've."

He put her on the Apache's horse, got behind her, and they rode to where he had tethered the roan.

Before they started for the camp, she spoke. "What happened between us, Slocum—it'd be best to leave back there, with the Apache."

"What do you mean?"

"Well, we did get carried away. I think it'd be best if Brogan did not know about us. He's a jealous man, as you probably noticed."

"Yes, I've noticed." Slocum's voice was dry.

Back in the camp, Brogan, at the sight of her, let out a holler. He came up to her horse, his face worried. "Are you all right? What did that redskin bastard do?" He looked at her shrewdly, expecting the worst.

She nodded. "I'm all right. He knocked me out." She put her hand to the bruise on her forehead. "I suspect he hit harder than he had wanted. He couldn't do a thing with me after that. And Slocum came up fast."

Brogan looked searchingly at her face. "Then you're all right. I was worried sick."

She smiled. "Slocum didn't give him the time."

Brogan looked gratefully at Slocum. "We sure do owe you."

Slocum just shrugged.

"Well," Brogan said, "maybe it'll be easier traveling from here on. We should make the town of Locust Grove by sundown."

They rode most of the afternoon under a smiling, blue sky; the June grass stretching out was lush, green, and clean scented. Slocum, always cautious on the trail, would sometimes climb a rise and using his field glasses, survey the land behind him.

The second time he did it, he picked up a lone rider whose contours seemed familiar. He studied the rider, then recognized the sinewy cowboy as Berne's sidekick. What the hell would he be after? Slocum's face hardened. An avenger? It was possible. He watched. No, the cowboy was not tracking, and he was a half mile south of their trail, just riding to Locust Grove. But he did seem to be in a hurry; his horse was stretched out. Did it mean anything?

5

When they rode into Locust Grove it was sundown, and the main street was busy with cowboys, drifters, drunks, gunfighters, and ruffians. Rosemarie was tired, hurting with a slight headache, and wanted to rest. Brogan, too, was weary and saddle sore. They took rooms at the hotel and retired for the night.

Slocum felt like a drink or two, and decided to relax at the Blue Star Saloon. He walked down the broad, dusty street, pushed in the batwing doors, and looked at the densely packed room of drinkers, gamblers, and several party women.

He strolled to the bar and watched the bartender dishing out drinks; he was tall, beefy, with gray eyes and a secret smile, as if everything around him had a comic touch. Someone at the bar called him Black Jack. Slocum waited patiently. Black Jack finally came to him, his eyes shrewd. "What's your poison?"

"Whiskey."

Black Jack poured a drink, and put the whiskey bottle in front of Slocum. There was a lull at the bar, so the bartender leaned on the counter. "Just ride in, mister?"

"Yeah. And the town's jumpin'."

Black Jack's gray eyes surveyed the noisy drinkers, and

41

his lips curved up. "Friday night. They come in from ridin' in the hot sun all week, and they're thirsty, lookin' for fun, ready to drink, and ready to fight. Some ready to croak. Bad night, Friday."

Slocum laughed and lifted his glass. "That's the way the world goes."

"What's your handle?"

"Slocum."

Black Jack's eyes wavered for a moment, as if the name struck a chord.

"Ridin' through, Slocum?"

"To Silver Fork."

"Brogan's country," said Black Jack. He looked fixedly toward the far end of the saloon.

Slocum drank his whiskey, then turned and followed the bartender's glance. Four cowboys, a tough, rugged pack, were sitting at the table, drinking. For a moment, Slocum wondered if Black Jack was telling *him* something or telling *them*. One of the cowboys, a young man with broad shoulders, wearing a black, porkpie hat, was looking right at him. Slocum didn't know if the look was hostile; he shrugged and poured another drink.

Just then snarling sounds came from one of the card tables. Players at that table rushed to the side of the saloon, leaving two men with guns in their holsters facing each other.

The saloon went silent.

One man with a bald head and dark moustache, rubbed his jaw and drawled, "So, if you lose the pot, the winner is crooked. Is that the way you figger it, Eddie?"

"You play a cheatin' game, Joel, and this time I caught you."

Eddie was small and muscular, with gray eyes that gleamed excitedly. He had just lost a big pot, and chose to believe Joel's crooked play did it. He wasn't going to let it go.

Joel, a young, attractive man, prematurely bald with a dark moustache, was flushed with anger, but controlling himself. "I know you're a sore loser, Eddie. I'll give you a chance to pull them words back."

Eddie glared, past the point of recall. "I know a tinhorn cardsharp when I meet one."

"That's it," said Joel.

They stared at each other and went for their Colts, pulling at the same time. The sound blasted the saloon, and the force of the bullets knocked them both down. They lay there and blood began to ooze.

"Sonofabitch," said Eddie, putting his hand to his shoulder. "I'm bleedin'."

"What the hell do you expect if you pull your gun, you dumb bastard," said Joel, looking at his side where the blood was starting to soak through his shirt.

Black Jack signaled a couple of his men, who took the wounded players out of the saloon and headed for Doc Finley's place.

The saloon went quickly back to normal, folks talking, drinking, and playing cards, as if nothing much had happened.

"That's it, Slocum, never a dull moment on Fridays." Black Jack grinned and went to another customer.

Slocum nodded and looked around.

The women were dressed in short, red dresses with ruffles, showing plenty of leg and thigh. The one near him, talking to a cowboy, had her back to him; with her rounded butt, she looked like a work of art. Slocum watched her. When she turned, however, he chilled off; her face showed the wear and tear of a hard life of drinking.

He sighed, and thought of Rosemarie, over at the hotel, probably sleeping by now.

Then he heard the voice. "Are you Slocum?"

The man who had come to his elbow had a rugged face with slitted, brown eyes, heavy brows, his black hat worn low; he was one of the four tough men who'd been sitting at the far table.

"That's me."

"Friend of mine wants to talk to you, mister." He jerked his finger at the table where the man in the black porkpie hat was sitting.

"And who would he be?"

"Easy to find out. Just go over there."

The tone of the gunfighter didn't please Slocum. "S'pose I didn't care to find out?"

Surprise lit the brown eyes. "I don't think it'd be smart."

Slocum did some thinking. The man was a touch hostile, and if he had to, he might pull his gun. But he was an underling, the main man was the one with the porkpie hat. Why did Black Jack cue the four men at the table? How'd they know his name? Was there a lineup against him? And what could be their business with him?

He strolled through the smoky, whiskey-smelling saloon toward the far table. When he reached it, the cowboy in the porkpie glanced at the other men. To Slocum's surprise, they stood and walked to the bar, where they turned to watch.

"Sit down, Slocum."

He took a seat and sat facing the young, good-looking cowboy with a strong face, and clear eyes that seemed a bit hunted.

"Where's Brogan?" the cowboy asked.

Slocum started. Another one of them, a gunfighter out to shoot Brogan to hell and back? They kept coming out of the woodwork. After the gold?

"Who's Brogan?" Slocum said, straight-faced.

"The cowboy's eyes iced. "Mister, you know him. You been travelin' with him."

"How would you know that?"

"I know plenty about you." The cowboy stared at him strangely, but Slocum did not feel hostility.

"What do you know?"

"You're a hired gun. You been protecting Brogan—all the way, almost from Tucson."

"And how would you know that?" Slocum drawled, wondering if he would face a shoot-out. They were four guns, he'd never stand a chance. But somehow he didn't think this cowboy was eager for a showdown. Something else was biting his ass.

"Why in hell would you hire your gun to a mean dog like Brogan?" the cowboy asked.

"Brogan, a mean dog? I don't see him like that." Slocum thought about it. "The truth is, I'd seen some Apache tracks and he had a girl with him, so I hired out more to protect his niece, Rosemarie, than him."

"His niece." The cowboy's voice was bitter. "She's his niece like you're my uncle."

Slocum's eyes slitted. This cowboy put his finger on it. Brogan had never treated her like kin.

"Well, who is she if she's not his niece?" Slocum demanded.

The cowboy looked away, then back to Slocum. "She's my ex-girl, my ex-sweetie. The girl I had hoped to marry. That's who she *was*."

Slocum stared. "Who the hell are you?"

"I'm Seth Brogan."

Slocum was jolted. He looked around the saloon, at the drinkers, the gamblers, the three cowboys at the bar.

"Well, Seth, I'm not sure I'm getting this clear. You

tellin' me your father stole your girl?"

"My father?" Seth ground his teeth and looked down. "Look, Slocum, I don't want to get into a lot of things that aren't your business. The main reason we haven't gunned you down is because you helped Rosemarie. I know about the Apaches."

"How would you know that?"

Seth just smiled.

Then Slocum remembered the sinewy cowboy, Berne's sidekick in Redstone, the one who had been following their trail, then galloped ahead. He had got to Locust Grove and talked to Seth, giving him the lowdown on what had happened.

So what did it mean? It meant that Seth was trying to kill his own father! The idea was heinous. He spoke in a hard voice. "Are you behind the gunmen trying to mow Brogan down?"

Seth looked away.

"Your own father?" Slocum persisted.

Seth turned back. "Rosemarie is *not* his niece, and he is *not* my father." He poured a drink and tossed it off. "He's my stepfather."

Slocum watched him. "Well, your stepfather. Why in hell do you want to execute him?"

"Because that's what he and his dog of a son, Gillis, have been trying to do to me."

Slocum reached for the bottle on the table and poured himself a drink. This was one mad muddle. "Why should Brogan try that? Just because of Rosemarie?"

"No, he's greedier than that. He wants the Silver Fork ranch, which belonged to my mother. She died. I own half of it, and Brogan got half from the will. She died," he repeated, his eyes glittering. "How'd she die? By accident, one day while riding with Brogan. A snake bite. A snake bite," he hissed a second time. He reached for the whiskey and drank. He was a young cowboy with strong feelings. "That's what Brogan said. I'm not satisfied it was an accident. This hombre, Brogan, is loco about Rosemarie, he wants her. He wants the ranch. I'm the sticking point. He wants me out." He grinned ferociously. "Am I right to go after Brogan? Then there's Gillis, his mangy son, gunning for me, too."

Seth waited calmly for Slocum to digest it all.

Then he smiled, but his eyes were cold. "So you see, mister, you're on the wrong side. And the sooner you get the idea, the better your chances, because you're in the middle of a feud. Gotta make up your mind where you want to be— with Brogan and against me, or the other way."

Seth stood up. "I'm giving you time to think about it." He paused. "I s'pose Brogan might be at the hotel. Trouble is Rosemarie would be there, too, and I don't aim to get her upset. Plenty of time to settle with Brogan. If not today, then another. We're ridin' out now. I've got other fish to fry."

He sauntered past the bar, and his men, taking a last look at Slocum, still at the table, fell in behind him. They went out the swinging doors.

Slocum sat there thinking. Seth had really scrambled the picture he had in mind of Brogan and of Rosemarie.

What sort of woman was she, anyway? If Seth was to be believed, she'd be a strange one. Up to now he had admired her guts, her style, the way she handled herself. If Seth was to be believed. But maybe he was a liar. Before today, Slocum knew nothing about him. Was Rosemarie really his ex-girl? Was Brogan really loco about the lady? He seemed plenty jealous. If that was true, was the rest of his story true? All that about his mother's death—was Brogan really behind that? Sounded farfetched. Money seemed to be at the bottom of it.

It was hard to take a position until he found out more.

He lifted his glass and drank. His first impulse was to say a plague on both your houses and just ride off for Phoenix, but perhaps he wasn't free to do that, not anymore. He had shot a couple of men in Seth's gang, men out to mow Brogan down. Seth wasn't going to let him move out that easy.

Then Slocum thought of Rosemarie, one scorched filly. He remembered how she had come at him after the fight with the Apache. But why would she give Seth the boot for Brogan, an older man? Well, that needn't be a mystery— many a woman found older men more interesting than the inexperienced yearlings with nothing in their jeans.

Slocum felt involved with her, too. What would happen to her? Two men, Brogan and Seth, hot after her. Things didn't look so great for her, either.

He thought about it a bit more, then started to walk toward the door. Black Jack, behind the bar, was watching him. On impulse Slocum stopped and went over. The barman looked at him with his secret smile. "Seth driving you to drink, cowboy?"

His voice was careful. "Were they expecting me, Black Jack?"

The barman nodded. "They knew you were comin'."

"And you let them know."

"I let you know, too, Slocum." He mopped the bar with a towel. "I knew there'd be no shootin'."

Slocum looked into the smiling gray eyes and he had to laugh. He liked a smiling man. Considering what a man went through, it was something of a triumph for him to keep his sense of humor. He leaned on the bar, and said, "But you never really know, Black Jack, if there'll be a shooting, do you?"

Black Jack's smile suddenly disappeared.

Slocum walked out into a street beginning to settle down to nighttime silence, except for a wandering cowboy.

At the hotel, the clerk gave him his room number, and from the register, he could tell it was next to Rosemarie. He felt an impulse to visit her, but she had gone through a hard day and was probably sleeping deeply.

In his own room, he walked to the window and looked out. The moon was high and throwing down plenty of light on the street, and on the jagged peaks of the distant mountains.

Everything seemed calm.

But that was just surface stuff, Slocum felt.

A soft knock on his door. Slocum scowled, he had heard no footsteps on the stairs. Could it be Rosemarie? But he didn't take chances; he pulled his gun, quietly gripped the doorknob and jerked the door open.

It was Brogan, who looked startled at the sight of Slocum's gun.

Slocum slipped the gun into its holster. Brogan took a deep breath. "Bit skittish, aren't you, Slocum?"

"You never know who's outside your door." Slocum's voice was grim.

Brogan nodded. "That's how you keep breathin' in these parts." He came in the room, walked to the open window, and looked up and down the street.

"Couldn't fall asleep; too restless," he said. "Got any liquor?"

"Nothing here."

Brogan turned again to the street.

"Looking for someone?" Slocum asked.

"Wouldn't surprise me if a couple of my boys show up."

"Expecting Seth?"

Brogan looked startled and examined Slocum with sharp eyes. "Wasn't thinkin' of him. Maybe you saw him in the saloon?"

"Yeah, he came in."

That jolted Brogan. "He did? How'd you know it was Seth?"

"They invited me to his table."

Brogan stared. "Who invited you?"

"One of his guns."

"You talked to Seth?"

"Well, he talked to me."

Brogan looked out the window at the moon-drenched crags on the mountain. When he turned back, his face had a broad smile. "You can be sure of one thing, Slocum, whatever he told you was a pack of lies."

Slocum rubbed his chin, but said nothing.

Brogan looked relaxed and sat in the chair, still smiling. "Got a smoke?"

Slocum fished out a cigarillo, and Brogan lit it with a lucifer, blowing out the smoke.

"Seth has a lot of funny ideas percolating in his head," Brogan said. "His ma died, got bit by a snake. It rocked that poor boy. Never the same after her death, crazy ideas. Figgered that I did his mother in. Imagine that— my own wife. That I did it to get the ranch." He stopped, blew smoke, and watched it drift. His eyes were dreamy. "Seth was all tangled up with Rosemarie, wild about her. Well, he became peculiar, so naturally she turned away from him. Turned to me for a shoulder to lean on. So then he got the funny idea that I stole his girl. Stole his girl."

Suddenly Brogan stopped and studied Slocum. "He did tell you junk like that, didn't he?"

"More or less," Slocum said.

Brogan stroked his chin nervously. "And he took you in, I'm sure of it. But don't be in a hurry to believe that coyote. He's gone a bit loco."

Brogan waited for Slocum to speak, but he said nothing.

Brogan's face hardened. "I tell you, Slocum, I believe it's Seth behind those gunmen who tried to mow me down back on the trail. He's the one. I thought at first it might be thieves after gold. But now I realize it was Seth's hired guns. He's out to gun me." He stared hard at Slocum. "Do you believe me?"

Slocum nodded. "No reason not to. I figured him a bit wild."

Brogan clasped his hands and studied them. "So he brought his gunfighters into town, did he? How many?"

"Four, including him."

Brogan got up, walked to the window, and looked out. "Tell you a secret. I've been expecting a loco deal like this from Seth. And I been preparing. Some of my boys will be riding into Locust Grove. Expected them today."

Slocum stroked his chin thoughtfully. He couldn't make up his mind about Brogan, nor for that matter, about Seth. One of them had to be a fantastically good liar; trouble was he couldn't tell which.

So he said, "There's nothing to worry about. Now, anyway. Seth and his hired guns rode outa town. They're gone."

Brogan looked pleased. "That's good. Seth makes me nervous when he's nearby. My boys from Silver Fork should be here tomorrow. Then we'll take good care of Seth." He turned and spoke slowly. "Of course, you know, Seth is not blood kin. He's my stepson. And he's just gone dangerous."

6

Next morning, the three of them, Brogan, Rosemarie, and Slocum, were eating breakfast at Lucy's Café, plenty of eggs, bacon, biscuits, and coffee.

Slocum, on his second coffee, was feeling good. He had done no further thinking about the feud between Seth and Brogan. He'd see what happened. Meanwhile, he found Rosemarie delightful to look at across the table. Refreshed by sleep, her skin glowed, her cornflower-blue eyes were clear, her breasts thrust against a blue shirt; she was a young woman in her prime.

Brogan seemed distracted as he ate, his mind gnawing on some problem. He kept glancing out the window at the cowboys riding past.

Suddenly his face brightened, and Slocum, looking out, saw the six men riding down the broad street. The rider in front, a powerful cowboy, sighted Brogan through the window and turned to speak to the man behind him. The men continued to ride past the café, but the front rider turned his horse, and dismounted in front of the restaurant.

He came to their table and pulled a chair over. "Bring me some coffee," he said abruptly to the Mexican waiter.

"'Bout time you got here, Mire." Brogan's voice had a touch of complaint.

Mire didn't answer him, but grinned broadly at Rosemarie. "It's a pleasure to see you, Rosemarie."

She smiled politely, and sipped her coffee.

Mire looked critically at Slocum, then spoke to Brogan. "We got here as fast as we could."

"That coyote was in town last night," said Brogan.

Mire spoke casually. "We tracked him in, him and his boys."

Brogan frowned, not impressed.

The rancher jerked his finger. "This here is Slocum. I hired his gun. He gets $200 when we reach Silver Fork."

Mire stared hard at Slocum. "If he's workin' for you, he can join my bunch."

Brogan turned quickly to look at Slocum, unsure that such an arrangement would suit him. What he saw in Slocum's eyes made him speak quickly. "We'll see about that later."

Then, aware that he had not presented the newcomer, Brogan said, "This is Dick Mire, my foreman. He handles things—the invincible gun." He grinned suddenly. "A good man to have on your side when the shootin' starts. Like you, Slocum."

The remark that put Slocum on his level made Mire frown, and look more shrewdly at the green-eyed cowboy casually drinking coffee. He looked at his rugged face, powerful, lean body, the strong fingers, his well-used Colt.

"Where you from, Slocum?"

"Calhoun County, Georgia."

"Rebel." Mire grunted. "We got a lot of blue-bellies in the bunch. Hope that won't bother you."

"The war's over," Slocum said. He couldn't make up his mind about Dick Mire. A heavily muscled man, with a thick neck, hefty chest, fair, reddish skin, curly, light-colored hair, and piercing, gray eyes in a round face. Though his body was strongly masculine, his face seemed almost boyish. A dangerous man, ready to prove himself, ready to go the limit to do it.

"There's plenty for who the war's not over," Mire said, scratching his cheek. "I was forced to put away some of them, myself."

Slocum stared at him. "Is that right?"

"Don't like a sore loser," said Mire.

Slocum nodded. "Tell you the truth, Mire, I don't care for a sore winner."

Mire's eyes narrowed but he said nothing.

Brogan chafed. "Forget the war. We got immediate problems. It's what Seth's doin' that interests me."

Mire looked thoughtfully at Rosemarie. "He's got three gunfighters and he keeps moving around. Not easy to get him to stop and talk."

Brogan looked at Rosemarie. "Do me a favor, honey. We need some jerky, we still got a way to go before Silver Fork." He reached into his pocket and gave her money.

She took it and stood up. "I hate to leave such pleasing company."

"And we hate to see you leave," said Mire, grinning hard.

They watched her go out the door, a comely figure, each man with his private thoughts.

Then Brogan said in a harsh voice, "They been tryin' to shoot my head off."

Mire picked at his teeth. "Who?"

"Some damned gunmen. We had a bad time on the trail from Tucson. Gunfighters in Redwood, Apaches. Hard to get a good night's sleep."

"I tole you to take some guns along," Mire said.

Brogan had wanted to travel with Rosemarie alone, didn't think trouble would happen.

Then Brogan looked thoughtfully at Slocum. "Seth came in last night and talked to Slocum. Told him a lot of stuff, you know, his crazy ideas, like I took his girl. Blames me for his ma's death. The boy's gone a bit loco."

Mire nodded. "Trouble is, some folks believe him." He stared hard at Slocum. "You believe him, mister?"

Slocum stroked his chin. "I stopped most believing when I got to be the size of a billy goat."

They laughed.

Brogan had been thinking. "Dick, maybe you ought to go find Seth. He's not sittin' and waitin'. The quicker you find him, the easier I'll sleep."

He turned to Slocum. "If a man thinks you want to knock him out, he's goin' to try and hit you."

Mire jerked his finger at Slocum. "What about him? Want him to join the bunch?"

Brogan thought about it. "No, you go after Seth with the boys. We'll go on like we were, with Rosemarie. Slocum's a good gun and tracker. I feel all right with him."

Mire gave Slocum a crooked smile, and stood up. "See you around."

As he started toward the door, one of the men who'd been eating at the counter turned and stood. He had a gun in his hand.

"You ain't goin' anywhere," he said.

There was a deathlike hush.

"Which one is Dick Mire?" he asked.

Slocum studied the man. He was a slender cowboy, with a narrow face, small nose, and a mouth that was a tight line of red. He didn't seem to know which of the three was Dick Mire, and his glance skipped from face to face.

He spoke first to Slocum. "Who are you?"

"Mister, I don't know who I am when a gun's pointing at me. Just lower it a bit, then we may talk."

"I'll lower it when the time is right." His gaze shifted.

"Are you Dick Mire?" His voice was hoarse.

"I'm standing here, minding my own business," said Mire, who didn't like the glint in the polecat's eyes. He smiled. "Maybe your gun is causing a memory loss."

"You're damned persnickety for a man facing a gun."

"What's all this about, mister?" Brogan sounded testy. "Things getting so bad you can't eat in a café without some-one pulling a gun on you."

The slender cowboy gritted his small, yellow teeth. "I heard someone use the name Dick Mire. I know you ain't Mire 'cause your age is wrong. But you're goin' to tell me, otherwise I'll put a bullet in you."

There was a silence, nobody in the café moved.

"It won't kill you, but it'll hurt you. Now talk, which one is Mire?"

Brogan drew a deep breath, he'd been thinking hard. "Tell us why you're lookin' for him."

Again a silence. Then the cowboy spoke. "Sure I'll tell you. I'm Lee Brown. Dick Mire shot my brother Joe, in Amarillo eight months ago. Fight over a saloon girl. I been lookin' for Mire. Thought I'd never catch up, even gave up lookin'. Then I'm sitting here eatin' and I hear the name, Dick Mire, behind me. It hit me so hard, I couldn't think. Then, when I did turn, his name didn't come up again. Now, you ready to talk?"

Brogan smiled broadly. "I get it. Well, sure, I did men-tion Mire, but he's not here. He's expected in town, a little later."

The cowboy stared at him. "You're a liar." He stepped back. "I don't aim to shoot an innocent man, but you're forcin' me. Reckon I'll have to shoot you all."

"You'll hang, Lee," Brogan said.

"I'll take my chances. Long as I get the right man." He cocked the trigger. His eyes went over all three, then fearful one might try for his gun, he said, "Throw your pistols. Take 'em out careful."

Slocum threw Mire a glance; the cowboy's gun, Slocum had noted, was pointed at him. Slocum took out his Colt and shoved it at the cowboy's gun hand, a gesture that confused him for a moment, but it was all Mire needed. His hawk eyes had picked up Slocum's signal and his gun came out lightning fast, spurting fire. The bullet hit Lee Brown, flinging him back, his gun firing at the ceiling. He fell with a bullet in his chest, the blood starting to leak. His eyes glazed.

"Sonofabitch," he muttered, and his gaze went to Slocum, who, he felt, was the cause of his death.

They watched him. He groaned softly, then died. The people in the café came forward to look at him.

Slocum turned to Mire. "I expected you to hit him, not kill him."

Mire's lip curled. "He was goin' to kill us, mister. You'd a done the same thing."

"Don't worry about it, Slocum," said Brogan. "It was him or us. Hey, Mire, so you shot his brother. Do you remember him?"

"Yeah, I remember. A whore in Amarillo. Good looker. She was with him and smilin' at me, the drunken polecat didn't like it. One word led to another so we pulled guns. A fair fight." He took his hat off and rubbed his scalp. "You shoot someone, his kin comes after you, don't matter if it was a fair fight or foul."

Slocum had to admit the truth of that. He, too, found himself facing gunmen who came out of the woodwork, claiming he'd killed their kin. Those were the most dangerous of showdowns—most of these gents wanted to shoot first and explain later.

"Well, thanks, Slocum. Reckon your smart move saved our hides." Mire started for the door.

"I'll go along with you," said Brogan. He turned to Slocum. "Maybe you can go see how Rosemarie is doin' at the general store."

He then spoke to the Mexican waiter looking at the dead cowboy. "Take care of that, amigo."

Slocum watched the waiter and a customer carry the dead cowboy outside and throw him over his horse. The customer, holding the reins, walked the horse west, and the Mexican came back to the café. He scrubbed the floor, then looked at Slocum who just shrugged. Life in the territory was like that: live fast and die fast. The dead cowboy seemed no more than eighteen.

Slocum drank the coffee still in his cup. His mind went back to Dick Mire. A tough hombre, fast; maybe under that sour front he had a heart of gold, but it was not easy to spot, and what's more, the man liked Rosemarie. But so did they all. Slocum liked her, too. Seth said she was his ex-sweetie. And what the hell was she to Brogan? All things to all men. He remembered how she came at him after he speared the Apache. She had figured she'd be a dead pigeon when the Apache got through with her. Was that why she came at him, body and soul?

Well, maybe he'd mosey up to the general store and talk to Rosemarie, try to find out a few things. Like who was telling the truth, Seth or Brogan? He had got himself in the middle of a feud. And if he had to use his gun, he didn't want to point it at the wrong man.

Brogan and Mire walked down the dusty, broad street under the warming sun until they reached the saloon. Brogan looked at the rocking chairs on the porch outside the saloon. "Let's sit a couple of minutes."

Mire glanced at him, sat down, lit a cigar, and began to rock gently.

Brogan looked up the street at a cowboy loading supplies in a wagon in front of the general store. "Hey, Mire, I had been expecting Seth would be pushing daisies by this time." His eyes burned. "Instead he's got gunmen trying to blast my head down the trail. Lucky Slocum came along."

Mire shrugged. "I told you, when you left, to take a couple of the boys with you. You and Rosemarie can ride back with us to Silver Fork."

"Dammit, Mire. You keep thinking about Rosemarie."

"Who doesn't, Brogan?" His manner was jocular.

Brogan's face hardened. "Your job is thinking about that polecat, Seth, before he does real damage."

"We'll take care of him."

"Won't be easy. He's got good men."

"It won't help."

Brogan studied Mire and smiled broadly. "You got cojones, mister." He had seen Mire shoot and figured him the best gunfighter in the territory. He hired his gun because he wanted the best.

Brogan thought back to the café. "What do you think of this Slocum?"

Mire's face was expressionless. "Not much."

Brogan looked surprised. "He did all right back in the café."

"Did he?"

"Well, he coulda told that lunatic *you* were Dick Mire. The gun was pointing at him."

Mire nodded. "Yeah, he did the right thing."

Brogan stared at him. "Would you do it, with a gun pointing at your gut?"

Mire smiled languidly. "If he's a fool, must I be one?"

Brogan smiled. "That's why I like you, Mire. You're more of a bastard than me."

Mire didn't smile, but he looked pleased.

Brogan stayed on the point. "Slocum also did the trick. Bamboozled that loco so you could get a shot at him."

"So what?"

"He thought of it, not you."

Mire drawled. "That boy had his gun pointing at Slocum. I'da shot him after he fired."

"You would, too," Brogan said. "Okay, get your boys and nail Seth. I don't like him running loose."

"We'll take care of him. Just a matter of time."

Brogan watched Mire, a cocky gun, stand up, stretch, then saunter into the saloon.

7

Brogan lit up a cigar, leaned back in the chair, and relaxed. As he smoked he felt meditative, then looked up the street to see Rosemarie, who had gone first to the hotel and was now walking toward the general store.

He watched her walking like a beautiful woman walks, stepping light; a stunning figure, breasts pushed out. A girl like that, he thought, to be wasted on Seth, that miserable yearling. A crime. From the first moment he had sighted Rosemarie, Brogan remembered, he had wanted her. That's how things worked with him, and what Brogan wanted he went for. Like the Silver Fork ranch; he'd got that because he wanted it.

He was not a man who rushed wildly at the object of his desire. He believed in foxy ways. The fox knew how to throw false scents, how to play tricks, and that's how he did it.

His mind skipped back to Lottie, his wife, Seth's mother. He had married Lottie for the Silver Fork ranch. She'd been a rich, lonely, good-looking widow with a grown son. Even in those days, he had to work against Seth, who didn't believe he was honest, didn't like him.

Seth had the right instincts, Brogan thought grimly. He

would tell Lottie that Seth was jealous. And she'd say, yes, but it was natural, the son hated to lose his mother to the stranger. Of course, in ranch matters, Brogan couldn't help but favor his own son, Gillis, which sharpened the hard feelings on the ranch.

But it was when Seth brought Rosemarie, a girl he was sweet on, to the ranch, that clinched things. Brogan watched the girl with sleek skin, honey hair, and a body that made you want to eat her up. And she had style. The more he saw of Rosemarie, the more he ached for her. He began to crave the girl, and thought of nothing more than how to dump Lottie and get Rosemarie.

What was the deal? Get rid of Lottie, keep the ranch, and get the girl. How to do it without catching hell? He thought about it hard.

Then fate took a hand.

He remembered the day he went riding with Lottie. It was hot, the sun blistered the rocks, the horses sweated, and when they came to the rivulet, they stopped. The horses drank. Lottie took water into her palms, patted her face to cool down. They sat in the nearby shaded, dense thicket for a while and talked. Lottie had been acting a bit remote lately, and he wondered if she'd picked up on his feelings about Rosemarie.

Finally she said, "I'm worried about Seth. He's gotten restless."

Brogan scowled, he often did when Seth's name came up. "That boy never liked me."

"I wouldn't say that, Jim. He's young." She leaned back. She had a pleasing face with hazel eyes and full lips. She was wearing a short-sleeved yellow shirt with a matching skirt and riding boots; although an older woman, she still had her figure. "You see it often, sons hate to lose their mothers," she said.

Brogan's face was grim. "It's more than that. He's got something against me."

"You think so?"

"I can tell. He looks at me with a mean eye."

She glanced at Brogan. "He's got a girl now, Rosemarie. Maybe his energies will turn to her."

"Do you think Rosemarie likes him?" he asked suddenly.

"What kind of question is that? Of course she does."

Brogan turned to look at the far-off mountain peak poking through its nest of clouds. "Young ladies never know their own minds."

Her eyes glinted frostily. "Tell the truth, Jim. It seems to me you're caught up by Rosemarie yourself. Every time she comes into the room you light up. Don't you?"

"That's ridiculous, Lottie."

"But it's true, isn't it?"

"You're the one I care about." He leaned toward her.

She raised her hand to bar him. "I think what you care about is Silver Fork."

He stared in disbelief. So she knew. What would she do about it? It was a dangerous situation. If she really understood what he was thinking, she could tell him to get on his horse and keep riding, anytime. Then what? He'd be an ex-rancher, and what was more pathetic than that?

It was then he saw the snake slithering behind her, near the canteen. Lottie was in its path, but the snake wouldn't strike, not unless she made a move.

He thought quickly. "Reach me that canteen, please, Lottie."

She reached for it, and the snake struck, a lightning move, hitting her arm. She was jolted. She looked at the writhing snake, at her arm. She could see the bite of the poisonous fangs.

He stood up and calmly shot the snake. Then he watched her.

"Get me to Dr. Smith, quick," she said.

"Sure," he said, and walked casually to his horse. He turned to look at her.

She watched him, a bit dazed. "Jim," she pleaded.

He got on his horse.

He came back alone thirty minutes later.

She was dead.

Then he took her into town, to Dr. Smith.

Thinking about it later, Brogan told himself it was the hand of fate, that the sidewinder would have got her anyway, and he was just destined to shake loose from Lottie.

But it was the best thing that could have happened. Lottie's will gave him a stake in the Silver Fork, he shared it fifty-fifty with Seth, who was a thorn in his side. Rosemarie began to smile at him. Before that, she'd been real careful. She seemed to lose her interest in Seth for some reason. And he began to campaign to wean Rosemarie from Seth, that pesky polecat.

It wasn't too hard, because Seth turned mean as hell. The death of his mother from snakebite made him wild. He didn't believe it. He'd look at Brogan with murder in his eyes. Somehow he guessed that his stepfather, in some way, had from the beginning played tricks to get the ranch and eventually had brought about the death of his mother.

Once he confronted Brogan. "Whyn't you suck out the poison?"

"I did," Brogan said.

Seth stared at him and knew he was lying.

Brogan figured it would be only a matter of time before Seth would demand a showdown. That's when he hired Dick Mire, a Tombstone gunfighter. He'd seen Mire in action at a Tombstone saloon. A bounty hunter, in a mean whiskey mood, pushed Mire, who was in his way. There were quick insults and both went for their guns. Mire's draw was a wonder to behold, and the bounty hunter went rocketing back with a hole dead center in his forehead.

After that, Brogan talked to Mire, offered him a fat proposition to come down to Silver Fork, and bring along four gunslicks.

In time, Brogan told him about Seth, but he tried to keep his intentions about Rosemarie secret.

Even meditating about Rosemarie made Brogan's nostrils widen with excitement. She was a prize, and he'd let nothing get between him and that filly.

Nothing.

Rosemarie had just finished shopping by the time Slocum walked into the general store. She had bought beef jerky, canned beans, and canned fruit. Slocum took the bag of food as they walked into the street.

" Let's bring this to the hotel and wait 'til Brogan's ready to ride," he said.

She glanced at him, and he wondered if that meant they had time for a fast laydown. The idea appealed to him, but it could be tricky if Brogan came along at the wrong time.

"That's what we'll do, Slocum, wait for him. On the porch."

Slocum looked down the street at a lone, sweaty cowboy riding into town, but he kept thinking about Rosemarie. She was playing a careful game. With Brogan nearby, she wasn't going to kick over the applecart. She might have a lot invested in him. Slocum didn't know what to believe about her. Seth had said Brogan stole his girl. But you don't steal a woman unless she wants to be stolen. And if that was true, then she either liked Brogan or liked the idea of Silver Fork.

All that could slip away, if she made a wrong move with him, who, to her mind, might be passing through, just a fast gun hired by Brogan to protect them 'til they reached the ranch.

They walked under the morning sun to the hotel situated at the end of town and sat on straightback chairs on the empty porch. Slocum gazed at the ramshackle hut in front of him and the stark rocks at the foot of the vast mountain stretching west.

He put the bag at his feet and looked at Rosemarie; she had taken off her brown hat and was shaking her honey-colored hair. She leaned back on the chair, looking morning fresh, her skin sleek, her blue eyes sparkling, her pink shirt pulled against her full breasts.

He was thinking it would be nice to get her up in the room, but it wouldn't be easy. He decided not to think about it.

Instead he drawled, "You know what surprised me?"

She looked at him. "I didn't think much surprised you, Slocum."

"It's the way Brogan thinks about Seth. Not crazy about that boy."

She said nothing.

"At first, as I remember, Brogan talked about Seth as one of his two sons."

"Yes, there's Gillis—he's his real son. Seth is the step-son."

"What about this Seth? I hear you and he were very friendly at one time."

"Where'd you hear it?" She was frowning.

"From the horse's mouth."

She was astonished. "You met Seth?"

"Last night, while you were sleeping. He came into the saloon, looking for Brogan."

Her eyes blanked. She spoke slowly. "What'd he say?"

"He doesn't care much for Brogan."

She shrugged.

"But he seems to care about you, Rosemarie. Did so once, he said." Slocum watched her carefully.

"Yes, we were close."

"What happened?"

The lids slid down on her blue eyes. "Just got the idea that he might be wrong for me."

"Was that all?"

"That's plenty," she said. "Woke up one day and decided it might be a mistake to tie up with Seth." She brushed back her hair. "I liked him a lot, but then he seemed too young, like a wild colt. I'm interested in a mature man."

"Mature, like Brogan?"

"What's wrong with him?"

"I don't know. So he's the one."

She gazed at him with a secret smile. "Well, you might be the one, Slocum. But it doesn't take much to tell you're not a man who takes root."

"But Brogan is?"

"He's settled. He's got a big ranch."

Slocum leaned back in the chair, put his hands behind his head. "As I understand, the ranch belonged to Seth's mother."

Her eyebrows rose. "You've learned a lot in a short time, Slocum. His mother died, a terrible accident—snakebite. She died on the way to the doctor." Rosemarie sighed. "For some reason, Seth held Brogan responsible. Isn't that strange? I mean, it was a snakebite."

"Maybe Seth believes Brogan is not a man to be trusted."

"You know Brogan only two days, Slocum."

"Doesn't take long to know a man."

She stared at him. "So you don't trust Brogan?"

"Not an easy man to know. You can't see the thoughts behind his words."

"What's there to know? The way I see it, Seth has a lot of wild ideas. He believes Brogan somehow is at fault in his ma's death. He thinks Brogan is after his scalp, but that's not true. Brogan just wants to corner Seth, talk to him, make him see the light."

"Is that what Brogan wants—talk?"

"That's it. He wouldn't hurt him. Seth is his stepson."

Slocum shrugged. She didn't seem to get the picture. For some reason, Brogan was keeping it from her. Brogan hadn't told her that the gunfighters they had run into back on the trail were Seth's men. And Brogan didn't tell her that Dick Mire and his bunch were out to mow Seth down.

"Well," he said, "I don't think Seth is the sort of bronc who's going to lie down and let Brogan run over him."

There was a flicker of anxiety in Rosemarie's blue eyes. "I hate to see trouble between them. I feel that I might be the cause. I wouldn't like it."

There, that was why Brogan had got her out of the café, why he hadn't told her that he had Seth on target.

He looked up the street. Brogan was striding toward them.

He looked mean and ready to ride.

8

Seth stared into the dancing flames. There was something about fire that made you stare at it, but it made your brain go empty, too, and he didn't want that.

He had camped with his gunslicks on the trail to Silver Fork, a trail bristling with danger. If he didn't keep his head clear, it could get blown off by Brogan's gunfighters, led by that low-down Mire. They called Mire the "Invincible Gun," and Seth hated him almost as much as Brogan—just another horny dog with his eye on Rosemarie.

Seth started remembering her, but the pain hit, and he turned to look at his gunfighters eating around the fire. Leon, the left-handed gun and the fastest, a hunched-over sharpshooter; Arne, fearless in battle, with penetrating, gray eyes in a craggy face; Fast John, heavy-gutted with black hair, a laughing cowboy with a deadeye gun. They were hand-picked; he paid them well and they believed in his cause.

He was proud to lead them against the Brogan bunch—a force of evil.

Rosemarie—again he thought of her. In the early days, when he first brought her to the ranch, he'd been happy. He needed just such a woman to pull him out of the blues that had hit when Ma married Brogan. He distrusted Brogan even then, smelled him as a conniving polecat with an eye on Silver Fork, one of the richest ranches in Arizona, built with the sweat and tears of his father, who had died years ago in an Apache ambush.

The presence of Rosemarie on the ranch helped Seth, and his mood picked up, but then things changed. He began to notice the way Brogan watched Rosemarie, like a wolf watching a fawn. That critter was smitten, which he found hard to hide. Even Ma noticed. It bothered Seth but he didn't know what to do.

But then it didn't matter because things happened that went beyond his control. The way his mother died, that was a knockout blow; it put him into a fury. You couldn't force a snake to bite, but Seth held Brogan responsible. He should have killed the snake *first*, not afterward. And *why* didn't he get her to Doc Smith in time? Why? He believed that Brogan had married his mother under false pretense, and murdered her to open the way to Rosemarie.

As for her, she'd been spooked by something. He remembered the night he asked Rosemarie to ride out to the stream after Ma died. He had felt rotten and needed what Rosemarie could give a man at a time like this.

He looked at her, so lovely and desirable in the moonlight.

"Rosemarie," he said, "I'm all broke up because of what happened to Ma. I don't want to push you into a decision. I know you been thinkin' of me as one of your beaux, but these are bad times. I'd like for us to get hitched—the sooner the better. What do you say?"

There was a funny look in her bright, blue eyes as she studied him. "Seth, I know how you feel and I sorrow with you about your ma. That's why it hurts me when I consider what's in my mind."

He felt a cold shiver. "What d'ya mean? What's in my mind?"

She turned to look at the big cottonwood, its leaves glinting with moonlight. "It's this, Seth. I'm thinkin' I'm not ready to hitch up."

The jolt hit him. Something had been spooking her these last days and it had puzzled him. He put it down to the sudden death of Ma; it had spooked him, too.

He leaned forward, his voice intense. "Why aren't you ready? You look ready. You're bustin' out all over. You're the right age. It's the right time for you to hitch up."

There was sadness in her eyes. "I'm goin' to be straight with you, Seth, even though the time's not good. But I gotta be true. My feelings have changed. *I don't think we're right for each other.*"

The sinking feeling hit his gut. He started thinking about things. "Since when hasn't it been right? When did you start to think like that, Rosemarie?"

She looked embarrassed, like it was hard to handle her thoughts. "It's been there for some time, Seth. I was wantin' to tell you, but this thing happened to your ma. Couldn't talk about it then. But now that you're asking, I'm forced to tell you."

His thoughts were in a whirl, while he tried to find the reason for her change of heart. He thought of Brogan, now the honcho of the ranch. He thought of the way Brogan looked at Rosemarie, and of the way he talked to her.

"So you're forced to tell me now," he said sarcastically. "It's got nothing to do with Brogan, does it?"

She looked at him boldly; there was no fear in Rosemarie, he had to hand her that.

"Whatever I feel about Mr. Brogan has nothing to do with my feelings about you, Seth. I like you, but the truth is, I feel you're too young for me. I'm sorry if that hurts you, but it's my opinion. In the beginning, I thought it might be right between us, but I've changed my mind. I'm sorry."

He gritted his teeth. "It *is* Brogan, isn't it?"

"I don't rightly know," she drawled. "Might be him, might be someone else. In the spring a girl's fancy turns lightly to many a beau."

He glared. "I didn't figure you for a fickle filly."

She smiled. "Everyone's fickle, Seth. Even you, if you should see a lassie prettier than me."

His face went sulky. "That's a lie—I'm true blue. And you ain't." He leaned forward. "I'm saying that if Brogan hadn't turned up on Silver Fork, you'd still be sweet on me."

She flashed him an impish smile. "I'm still sweet on you, Seth. Never forget it. But I don't feel we're right."

He looked away. The desolation in his heart was overwhelming. He'd lost his ma, maybe the ranch, and now Rosemarie.

She saw the feelings in his eyes and it touched her.

"Don't take on so, Seth. There's plenty of girls who'd give their eyeteeth to get a hold on you."

He turned to her, his face grim. "Yeah, you ain't the only filly in the corral."

And that's how he left it. He walked away, his heart scorched. His rage flared against Brogan.

But that wasn't the only reason for turning on Brogan and his son, that woeful critter, Gillis.

But Seth wouldn't think of that, not now. His mind came back to the present, to the fire, to his gunfighters around him, to his deadly intent to destroy Brogan and Gillis.

He lifted the coffeepot, poured a cup, and drank. The taste was bitter, and he didn't know if it was the coffee or his thoughts.

The memory of Rosemarie had drained Seth, and after brooding a bit, he stood up to toss the coffee grounds into the fire. The bullet screeched past his ear. He dropped in shock and stayed flat. His men crouched, grabbing their guns, waiting for the next bullet.

But there was no further shooting. The hidden gunman might believe that his bullet had hit the mark. Maybe he was a crafty hombre who realized another shot would pinpoint his position.

From a crouch, Seth studied the land; the best ambush position would be the thick brush on the crest.

Seth turned to Lefty Leon, his best tracker; if anyone would find the bushwhacker, it would be him. "Lefty," he said. "Take a look. Most likely place is there." He jerked his thumb at the thick brush. "Be careful."

Lefty nodded, his fierce, dark eyes staring at the thicket, searching for movement. He was thinking of Dick Mire, hoping to find him. Not long ago, Dick Mire had shot Paddy, his sidekick, in a saloon fracas in Maricopa, and Lefty ached for revenge. He hitched his gunbelt, then crawled silently into the brush.

Seth turned to the other men. "How about that?"

"Brogan's men," said craggy-faced Arne.

"It was one of them," said John. "If the bunch were there, they'd all fire, to make sure."

"Why'd he stop after one shot?" Seth asked.

"Thought he did the job, the way you went down," said Arne. "A sharpshooter, one man, one target. That was you, Seth."

"May have been a sharpshooter, but he missed," Seth said. "But who would it be?"

"They're tryin' to hit you, Seth," John said, his dark eyes screwed up with thought as he patted his round belly. "They figger if they knock you out, the rest of us might quit."

"Yeah," Seth grinned. "So you'd best give me a lot of protection."

"That we'll do," said Arne.

The sun was starting down when Lefty Leon came back.

"Well, was it Mire?" Seth asked.

Lefty shook his head and looked grim.

The men waited.

"It was Gillis," he said.

There was heavy silence.

"You're sure?" Seth's voice was harsh.

Lefty shrugged. "I'd know his sorrel's prints anywhere. He was alone."

It didn't surprise Seth. It wasn't the first time Gillis had tried to cut him down. Like father, like son, they wanted him gone. That's how they hoped to get the ranch and get Rosemarie. Gillis, that sonofabitch.

Seth thought for a moment. "Lefty, do me a favor. Go after Gillis. He might lead you right into a rat's nest. I figger Brogan's somewhere on this trail. Don't know if he's coming with Mire or with Slocum. Meanwhile, maybe you could track Gillis and blow his head off. As a favor."

Lefty ran a hand over his black, curly hair and smiled. "Be glad to do it. That pasty-faced mutt. Hope to find Mire, too. Personally I'd like nothing better than to put Mire among his ancestors. Can't forget what he did to Paddy."

Seth put his hand on his shoulder. "If you spot the Mire bunch, get back here. Don't try to do it all. We'll hit them together."

Lefty nodded. Nothing he'd like better than to track that spoiled brat, Gillis, and put a bullet up his tail. Except to kill Dick Mire, the mangy dog who had shot Paddy Tavish, his best friend. Paddy gone forever just because Dick Mire didn't like the way a hand in poker turned out.

Lefty soon picked up Gillis's tracks. He stayed on them, moving carefully. From the horse droppings, he judged Brogan's son was ahead by two hours. Every so often

Lefty stopped and studied the surrounding terrain. After two hours of tracking, he noted Gillis had turned south at a fork in the trail. Lefty decided to scout the north fork before he went after Gillis. He climbed a crest and studied the land. A drift of smoke came up from a fire. A camp, half a mile away. Lefty whistled softly. Might pay to look: Dick Mire and his bunch were out there; it'd be a nice turn if he could locate the Mire bunch. Seth would like that. Lefty's jaw hardened. *He'd* like it even more. He thought of Paddy, his longtime sidekick, dead and gone, mowed down by Mire. "Mire—if ever a man needed killing it's that low-down varmint," Lefty muttered. The sky was turning orange, the breeze soft and scented. He'd hold off on Gillis for a time; a dumb critter like him was always easy to pick up.

Lefty moved toward the smoke.

Gillis Brogan cursed at the humidity, but he had nothing to complain about. Today had been a good luck day, because he'd done plenty. His dad would pat his shoulder, and say, "Good work, boy," after he told him about Seth.

Earlier, he'd been riding out of Silver Fork to crosstrail with his dad and the bunch. When he got to a knobby crest, thick with rocks and brush, he stopped to drink from his canteen and give his sweltering sorrel a breather. Then, on the odd chance he might catch sight of his dad's bunch, he looked through his field glasses at the surrounding land and picked up Seth and his gang camped at a fire.

His pulse jumped. Gillis wiped the sweat from his brow and considered the angles. It was a dangerous setup, but if he worked it right, his dad would be proud. Seth, at the fire, was a target waiting to be hit. Seth, whom he hated, stood in the way. Gillis remembered one night his dad saying, "We get rid of Seth, we get the Silver Fork free and clear. You'll be set for life, Gillis, you and the kids you'll have someday. And I'll get the missy Rosemarie, no strings. Can you think of anything better than that, boy? The mom's gone. We don't have far to go, do we?" Then his dad slipped him the wicked wink that told Gillis plenty.

Gillis was a sandy-haired yearling, with washed-out hazel eyes, and bad teeth that gave him a crooked smile. He hated Seth because he was a comely lad who could interest a beauty like Rosemarie, and because he stood in the way of the Brogans' grabbing the richest ranch in the Arizona Territory.

Twice before he'd tried secretly to get a bullet in Seth without luck. And Seth knew it; they were in a life and death feud.

And now he'd stumbled into this sweet setup. Seth, down there, a nice target; you hit him, nobody'd know, and his dad would give him a big hurrah for being smart.

Gillis felt the excitement rise in him. He surveyed the ground nearby; he'd shoot and make a fast getaway. But it could only be one shot—another would expose his position and they'd barrel down on him.

He pulled his rifle, cocked it, sighted, and waited. He needed more clearance on Seth to be sure. He could feel his heart thump in his chest. His mind was visualizing the hugs he'd get from his dad even as he held his breath. There, he squeezed the trigger! The rifle kicked against his shoulder; he saw Seth go down and heard the rifle crack echo against the crags. A wild exultation hit him. He had done it—Seth was gone.

He didn't wait around; those hombres might smell him out, come down on him. He crawled back to where he had picketed the sorrel, stuck his rifle in its holster, jumped on the saddle, and lit out for the trail west. He'd head off his father and give him the good news.

As Gillis rode, he felt a wild pride in his achievement.

9

Slocum's red neckerchief felt moist in the early heat. He took it off and mopped his sweating brow, then glanced at the sky. It was cloudless and the sun was laying there like a fried egg.

Since they left town he'd been riding a twisting trail in the front position, but now, for some inexplicable reason, Rosemarie brought her spirited horse in front of him, which left Brogan bringing up the rear. Slocum couldn't help but feel pleasure watching this well-shaped girl sitting straight and gracefully in the saddle. The rhythmic movement of her buttocks put him in mind of the aftermath of the Apache fight, when, excited by primitive battle, she had thrown her hot body at him. It had happened so fast, he didn't fully appreciate it.

Now with the heat warming his loins, he thought how nice it would be to get a replay of that passionate clinch, and his mind toyed with his chances. Not with Brogan sticking so close. That hombre eyed her as personal property; why else would he call himself her "uncle"? Might be amusing to push him on that angle, see him squirm, but Slocum would wait on that.

The sight of her enticing movement put a fire in his britches. Why in hell did she move in front of him anyway?

She was out to light a fire in him, that's why. The thought made Slocum smile.

After some heavy riding in the heat, they reached a stream.

"We might cool the horses and take a bite," he said.

"I'm goin' to bathe and cool down," she said, with an impassive look at the men.

Brogan stared. "That's not smart, girl. This is water, and bound to attract drifters and all such scum."

"That's why I've got two fast shooters with me," she said. "I'm sweaty and I'm going to bathe."

"She'll be all right," Slocum drawled. "But what we need is some fresh meat. Saw some rabbit tracks just back there, half a mile." He turned to Brogan. "You might pick that up."

Brogan's face hardened. "And what are you doin'?"

"I'll scout the terrain, make sure all is calm and quiet, so Rosemarie can bathe in peace."

Brogan didn't like it, but Rosemarie said, "Fresh cooked meat sounds good, Jim. Show Slocum how sharp you can shoot."

Brogan scowled, but decided to go with it. He swung over his saddle, kicked at his horse, and went back on the trail in search of rabbit.

They watched him ride.

"How far will he go?" Slocum asked.

"Far enough," she said cryptically.

He sighed. "Reckon I'll scout around. You can bathe."

"I'll bathe, but don't go far."

He wondered if her loins were in a turmoil, like his. She threw him a strange look, then with a few quick moves, stepped out of her clothes. He gritted his teeth because she didn't turn to him, as he expected, but started toward the stream. He watched the curve of plump hips, the slender waist, the movement of her buttocks as she sauntered to the water. She paused, perched like a nymph, then went into the gently swirling stream and lowered her body to her neck, but didn't let her hair get wet. Then she turned to him, her blue eyes wide open.

He grinned, waved, and started toward his horse.

"Where you goin', Slocum?"

"Scout the terrain, like I said."

"Just scout this terrain," she sang out.

"What d'ya mean?"

"Don't leave. I don't think we have much time."

He felt a jump in his britches. The sly little filly had been working a game all the time. Still, he thought, it'd be smart to reconnoiter the area, because Brogan was right, water brought all sorts to drink. But if she wanted play, the time was short, and that's what she might be thinking.

"You might like this cool water," she said.

"I might." He went close to the stream, left his Levi's on the edge, and walked in. She kept her distance. But when he came out, his body was in a state.

"Why do you remind me of a stallion?" she asked.

He grinned. "Because I feel like one."

She stepped out of the stream, dripping water, her breasts sleekly wet, her thighs comely; she was one luscious filly.

There was a nice grass spot near the brush. "Come with me. There isn't much time," he said. He brought their clothes along.

They came together in a feverish clutch. Her flesh was cool, it set him on fire. His hands went all over her, all her curves; her skin was sleek like wet satin. They went down to the grass, where she kissed him, her mouth went all over him. He felt the urgency, they came together as if pursued by demons. He pierced her and she let out a small moan. They grabbed each other and began a rhythm of powerful movement. Slocum, though caught up in the pleasure of the coupling, still was aware of the menace of interruption. The danger added spice. And then he felt the spasm of pleasure. Her body tightened and her arms held him fiercely.

When they were through, he slipped on his Levi's, then his boots.

"That was heaven," she said.

"Sure was," said the harsh, whiskey-roughened voice. "Don'tcha think so, Ethan?"

"Yeah, I think so, Luther," said another voice.

Slocum reached for his gunbelt.

"Don't do that, mister, or I'll put you in the real heaven." The speaker was coming toward them, a hombre with whiskers, in soiled buckskins. He was grinning, and his teeth were yellow. "Throw your gun now, gently. Though I imagine you're plenty tired, after that workout."

Slocum threw his gun.

"That's nice, isn't it, Ethan?"

The other hombre, Ethan, came from the thickets grinning comically. He, too, wore soiled clothes and whiskers; his flattened nose looked as if it'd been kicked by a mule.

They were staring at Rosemarie who was calmly slipping into her Levi's.

"What are you doin', missy?" asked Luther, picking up Slocum's gun.

"What's it look like?" She now calmly slipped her shirt over her breasts and started to button it.

Luther's face twisted malevolently. "A spirited filly, Ethan. Nuthin' pleases me more than a spirited filly."

"Yeah, but first things first, Luther." He turned to Slocum. "You been havin' a good time. You oughta pay for it."

"Yeah," said Luther. "If you dance you gotta pay the fiddler."

"But he wasn't dancin', Luther. He was doin' a sinful thing to this filly." Ethan grinned ear to ear, his nose taking a massive spread.

"Yeah, it's right that you pay for havin' a sinful good time, mister. So whyn't you give us your money?"

Slocum nodded, brought out his wallet, and held it, waiting for Ethan to reach for it.

Ethan made no move. He glanced at his sidekick. "He's a sly boots, isn't he, Luther? Jest throw it over here, mister." He raised his gun.

Slocum tossed the wallet. Ethan scooped it up, opened it, and whistled. "Hey, Luther, we hit the jackpot." He stared at Slocum. "Lucky at cards, are you, mister?" He grinned. "Well, they say, lucky at cards, unlucky at love. But you're doin' fine, both ways."

Slocum couldn't figure out these buzzards. Would they be happy with the money and go their way? Trouble was they had seen Rosemarie in the flesh, and they didn't look the type who could easily forget that. They might try something. If they did, it would mean the rope, if they got caught. Maybe they were ready to chance it. And what about Brogan? He might come barreling into this, then all hell would break loose. If the drifters shot one, they might shoot all. It wasn't hard to guess what they'd do first with Rosemarie. He nodded pleasantly. "Yeah, I been lucky. You boys are lucky, too. You've got some money. You might want to ride out somewhere and spend it."

Ethan, who had been greedily counting the money, nodded his head. "Might be smart, Luther. Let's hightail it."

Luther shook his head sadly. "Sometimes I wonder where they put your brains, Ethan."

Ethan stared at him. "Okay, if that worries you, we'll take their horses. They won't give us a hard time."

Luther's yellow eyes gleamed. "What about that filly?

You goin' just to ride off and leave her?"

"Not good to get mixed up with fillies," Ethan said gloomily.

Luther laughed. "He mixed up with her, and it looked good to me."

"You want to take her along?"

"Naw—she'd be too much trouble on the trail. We'll take her here."

Ethan considered that and a cunning grin slowly appeared on his broad face. "Luther, you gota lot of fun in you. Haven't I always said it? We let this hombre watch, jest like we watched him. We got his money. We give him the fun of watchin'. It's only fair."

That decided, they moved closer to Rosemarie, who all this time had paid no attention to them, as if they were insects on a cactus.

Slocum couldn't help but admire it, though it was not an attitude calculated to please these low-down scum.

Luther looked at her body with gleaming eyes. "Missy, I gotta hand it to you. Never seen a whore in Tucson who did as good as you."

She turned to stare at him and her hand went out like a rattler. The slap left a vicious print on his cheek.

Luther was jolted; there was a moment of shock, then his face twisted with hate.

Slocum's mind worked fast; he'd given up his gun easily, counting on the throwing knife in the secret pocket of his boot, but he had to wait for the right moment. Rosemarie, with that slap, had turned the hounds of hell loose, and he had to act.

He watched Luther stick the gun in his holster and reach out to grab Rosemarie with one hand, bringing the other back to punch her. She ducked. Ethan laughed gleefully, waiting for Luther to tear her apart.

"Go get her, Luther, eat her alive," he chuckled.

Slocum quietly slipped his hand to his boot, brought back the knife, and flung it hard. It caught Luther in the neck. He made the screeching sound of a slaughtered chicken, his hand going to his throat, trying to pull the knife free. Slocum followed the throw with a lightning move, jerking the gun from Luther's holster, and in the same motion firing at Ethan who was bringing out his own gun. Slocum's bullet smashed Ethan's chest and he stumbled back and fell.

Slocum looked at both men, Luther strangling in his own blood, Ethan twisting on the ground, struggling to breathe as his chest pumped out his heart's blood. Luther was slow to go, his eyes glaring with fear and fury.

Slocum scratched his head and looked at Rosemarie.

"'Bout time you did something, Slocum," she said coolly.

Slocum dragged the carcasses deep into the brush. They went back to their original site, near the stream.

Twenty minutes later Brogan rode up with a couple of rabbits hanging from the pommel of his saddle.

"It sure took a lot of scouting," he said irritably. He dismounted and held up his kill. "Fresh meat. But you don't know the kind of trouble I had to go through to corral these two jackrabbits."

Rosemarie glanced at Slocum. "Everyone gets his share of trouble, Brogan," she said.

10

Up in the orange-streaked sky, a buzzard soared, his big wings riding the south wind. To Mire, sitting in his camp and watching, the buzzard seemed to be in a hurry to reach his gruesome prey—a rendezvous with death. Mire smiled grimly; he felt a kinship to the deadly bird, because he himself was often in the presence of death.

He glanced at his men sitting and eating, surrounded by thick brush. Lennie, Sheehan, Allen, Beyer, all tough hombres, gunfighters that he'd culled from Tombstone, each with a record of kills. Brogan had told him he wanted such men to protect his cattle and even more, to hunt down Seth, his stepson. Brogan had got mighty nervous about Seth who had been trying to get a bullet in him.

In a way, Mire could scarcely blame Seth. Seemed like Brogan wanted everything Seth had—his mother, his girl, his ranch. Mire shook his head—such pure villainy appealed to him. In a way, you had to admire Brogan; most hombres were greedy in small ways, but Brogan did it big.

Mire had heard the story of Brogan's early days. He'd started as a small cattleman in southern Arizona. One day a cattle deal brought him into Maricopa. At the general store he saw the widow, Lottie, and her son, Seth, ordering feed, and the size of the order amazed him. He learned she was the widow of Larrimore and owned the Silver Fork, the richest ranch in the territory. He made a beeline for the lady; Brogan knew how to handle a rich, lonely widow. Didn't take long to marry her. When she died, he got part of the ranch. Now his target was Seth and the rest of the ranch. And he wanted Rosemarie, too.

Mire thought about Rosemarie and licked his lips: the filly with the lines of a thoroughbred. He liked to watch her move, and caught himself doing funny things with her in his mind. It had been a mystery why she ever tied up with a sawed-off cowboy like Seth, but she'd seen the error of her ways and now was running free.

Not completely free, he thought, because Brogan had a lasso out for her. Didn't he take her to Tucson—what the hell was that all about? He said she'd be visiting folks and that he had business in Tucson. All right—but the man had a thing for the filly, that was mighty clear. Brogan paid him for gunwork, but when it came to fillies, all was fair in love.

Mire always felt easy with the ladies; they liked him— fillies always like the macho man, and there was no mistake that he was macho.

Then Mire caught a movement in the brush; it was slight but unmistakable, it needed a look.

He waved his finger at Lennie, his ace scout, and pointed to the brush. The men stopped talking as Lennie moved silently into the brush.

Mire waited grimly, and it didn't take long for Lennie to come back, his gun out. With him was Lefty Leon, one of Seth's boys. He looked damned calm, nerveless.

Mire's eyes narrowed: he knew this critter, a bad hombre, good with a gun, they said. What was he prowling around for? Scouting their position, of course.

"Look what the cat brought in," he said.

The men laughed, and stared at Leon. Mire had four men

in his gang: Sheehan, pink-faced, had great power in his brawny body, a fun lover, he killed with a smile, no hard feelings; Allen, craggy, grinning, a killer with a kind heart; Beyer, piercing eyes in a broad face, who believed the bullet that could kill him had yet to be made; and Lennie, fast, a smart scout, solidly built, he moved like a cat.

"Well, Lefty Leon." Mire's smile was almost satanic. "I'm glad to see you. We were wondering where you boys were hiding and now you dropped in to tell us."

"Is that why I dropped in?" Leon said.

"Why else?" asked Mire innocently.

"He's wearin' his gun," Beyer pointed out.

"That's okay," said Mire. "Nuthin' to worry about."

The men smiled; it meant Mire had final plans for Leon.

"I'll tell you, Mire. I was drifting, looking for a place to sack out for the night, and here sneaks your scout, Lennie, showing me a gun."

"Lookin' for a place to sleep, Leon? The long sleep, Leon?"

Lefty's face hardened, but he said nothing.

"Well, he could join us," Allen drawled. "We don't aim to let you drift back to your boys and tell 'em where you spotted us. Maybe they'd hit us like sitting ducks."

Lefty's eyes traveled over the men watching him. "I was looking for Gillis; I'm sorry he's not here. I wanted to meet that brave hombre. He's the one who shot at Seth from behind a rock."

Mire looked surprised. "Shot Seth? Did he hit him?"

Lefty's lip curled. "He can't hit the side of a barn door, so how's he goin' to hit Seth?"

The men laughed.

Lefty stared at Mire. "At first we thought it might be you. You ain't much, but you're not the sort to shoot from behind a rock."

The men looked grimly at each other and watched Mire.

Mire slowly grinned. He didn't like the snotty words, but he was in no hurry. "Thanks, Lefty. You're right. It's not the way I'd meet Seth. Eye to eye, gun to gun, that's my way."

"So where the hell's fearless Gillis who crawled from under a rock to try and kill Seth?" Lefty asked. He knew Gillis was not with this bunch, but he was thinking, trying to make up his mind about something.

"He ain't here, as you can see," said pink-faced Sheehan. "So Seth's still breathin'. Wonder for how long."

Then Beyer let his hand fall over his holster and said, "Lots of folks are breathin', and you wonder for how long."

Mire scowled at Beyer, then turned to Lefty. "I'm glad about Seth. Don't like to hear somebody ambushed Seth. Not a decent way for him to go. He oughta get a fair shake."

"So whyn't you tell us where he is, Lefty?" said Lennie. "We'll give him a fair shake."

Lefty smiled, and from that smile they understood they'd never get a thing out of him.

"You better join us, Lefty. Don't want you wanderin' in this bad territory," said Mire.

"Thanks for the offer," Leon said, "but I don't think I'll stick around."

Mire stared, surprised at his nerve. "What's that?"

Leon looked coolly at the men around the fire. "Don't think much of the company. So I reckon I'll ride."

This time, the men didn't laugh.

Leon rubbed his chin. For a long time he had ached to draw against Mire. Not only because he'd shot Paddy Tavish, but because Leon always figured himself faster than Mire, though Mire had the big rep.

Leon had never been near-beat in a straight draw; it was why, back in the shooting club at Rimrock, they called him

"Killshot Kid." Now he might get a chance to draw against Mire, the buzzard who'd shot Paddy. Would he get out of this alive? It wasn't the best setup for a draw. If he beat Mire, nobody would draw; they'd be buffaloed, and he'd still have his gun out. He had a chance to make it.

Mire couldn't help but laugh softly at the brass balls of this cool hombre. "Don't think it'd be smart for you to leave, Leon. Might cost you a bullet."

"Like it did Paddy Tavish in Tombstone?"

Mire scowled. "Paddy? A mean dog." So that was it. Mire thought it strange that Lefty Leon would barge into his camp, practically looking for a showdown. "What's he to you, Leon?"

"A sidekick. And you cut him down for no reason."

Mire looked grim. "Lots of men get cut down for no reason." He paused. "Might happen to you. Now be smart, Leon. Tell us where Seth is settin'. Then you can drift on—wherever you want."

He grinned as he glanced at the other men.

They grinned back, aware he'd never let Leon get out alive, to come at them another time.

Lefty Leon's face was carved in granite. His eyes picked up the position of the bunch, just in case.

Mire stared hard at Leon, reading his intent.

"But if you're thinking of revenge for Paddy, there's nothin' I can do to stop you."

He paused, biting his lip. He didn't want a quick show-down with Leon, he wanted information, but this was a stubborn mule. He waited.

"Is there?" he persisted.

"Nothin'."

Mire stood up.

The men who'd been watching now backed away.

Leon scowled. Well, this was what he wanted. Mire was

a gunfighter with a record of killings as long as his arm, but that was Leon's drive, to match himself against the best. He thought of all the times he'd been cornered and got out with his killshot. A quick, dazzling move of his left arm, nothing wasted, bull's-eye to the target. That was why, looking into Mire's eyes glinting like blue stones, Leon felt the aura of invincibility. They were in the gunfighter's crouch, bent forward, waiting, then Leon felt the old nerve surge, his speed of draw and the touch of trigger, but he was already dead—Mire's bullet had pummeled through his brain. He went down not feeling a thing—he never knew he'd lost the draw.

Mire looked down at the fallen opponent. Leon's bullet had smashed the earth in front of him.

"Damn, he was fast," said Beyer. "Did you see that draw?"

"The bastard almost got me," Mire said. "He was faster than I thought."

There was a long silence while the men looked down at the dead man. Then Lennie spoke. "Well, Mire, we still don't know where Seth's bunch is."

Dick Mire smiled wickedly. "But the bunch is one man less."

After they reached the top of a rocky hillside on the trail, Brogan suggested they rest the horses, maybe have coffee. He told Slocum they were about seven miles from Honey Creek, the last town before Maricopa; it seemed a good time to take a break. It was then that Slocum spotted the lone rider.

He was headed directly for them and making no secret of it.

"Somebody wants to visit," he said.

Brogan looked nervous as he stared at the approaching

figure. He scowled, then his features broadened in a smile.

"That's my boy, Gillis. Don't know what he's doin' out here. Should be at the ranch." He turned to Rosemarie. "It's Gillis."

She shrugged and didn't seem to find that fact of much interest.

When Gillis reached them, he was grinning ear to ear. "Hello, Dad."

Brogan stared hard at him. "What're you doin' out here, Gillis? You're s'posed to be keepin' an eye on Silver Fork."

"It's all right, I've got Murph taking charge."

Brogan wasn't happy. "When are you goin' to learn to do the smart thing, Gillis? I don't want you runnin' loose." He paused significantly. "You could run into trouble." He jerked his finger. "This here is Slocum, he's a good gun."

Gillis was a pale, narrow-faced, awkward-looking young cowboy with washed-out blue eyes, blond eyebrows, and a bashful chin.

He ignored Slocum, his eyes hungry on Rosemarie. "Hi, honey, how you doin'?"

"Fine, Gillis, fine." She looked slightly bored. "It'd be nice if we could get back to the ranch in one piece."

"What's happening?" Gillis looked anxious.

"It ain't quiet out here," said Brogan. "You ain't answered me, why in hell are you running around? The best place for you is at the ranch."

Gillis looked sulky. "I was worried. I came lookin' for you, Dad."

"I got a fine gun protectin' me. It's you who should be worried. Prowling the country. You might catch hell." His eyes glittered. "You know Seth ain't happy with you."

Gillis looked at his father as if bursting to give him the news, but then, glancing at Rosemarie, he tightened his lips. Slocum wondered what was on his mind.

Gillis looked so peculiar that it irritated Brogan. "What the hell's the matter with you?"

Gillis took a slow, deep breath. "I'll tell you, Dad. I figgered you were due back. It began to worry me. So I decided to reconnoiter, see what I could find." Again he looked at Rosemarie and hesitated.

Brogan stared at him, aware that he had something in mind that might upset Rosemarie; he spoke hurriedly. "Look, we're just aimin' to stop for coffee, so whyn't you save the story of your adventures 'til then."

Gillis scowled, and felt cheated that he couldn't tell about his triumph, that he'd sent Seth to the big roundup in the sky, but he dared not buck his father.

So he sat down and chafed until the coffee was ready. He sipped his cup and ate some hardtack. He looked lecherously at Rosemarie, then curiously at Slocum.

"Where'd you get this man?" he asked his father.

Brogan gritted his teeth. "You don't listen, Gillis. I tole you. He's Slocum. He's got a fast gun, and doin' a good job. We figger it's smarter to travel small and let Mire and the bunch take care of our troubles."

Gillis couldn't control himself any longer, he was eager for his father's praise.

"That's what I've been tryin' to tell you, Dad. I've taken care of the troubles. You ain't goin' to be bothered by Seth. Not anymore."

Brogan stared. He didn't know whether to embrace his son or knock him on his ass. He had done good, but spilled the beans in front of Rosemarie.

She was frowning. "What's that about Seth?"

Brogan figured the cat was out of the bag, and it didn't matter anymore. She'd have to live with it.

"I said Dad wouldn't have to worry about Seth anymore." Gillis grinned.

"You shot him?" Brogan demanded.

"Yup." Gillis looked like a dog waiting for a pat of approval. But Brogan held off, watching Rosemarie staring at him and his son.

"You killed Seth? Why, for god's sake?"

Gillis looked bewildered; he knew that Rosemarie and Seth had gone steady, and almost gotten hitched. But he also remembered that they'd broken up. Why should she care what happened to him now?

Brogan stepped in hurriedly. "Rosemarie, I gotta tell you this. Those men shootin' at us on the trail were Seth's men. Seth's been trying to get me since his mom died. He blames me. I got tired of settin' around, tired of being his target. That's why I hired Mire. It worried Gillis, so he did something about it. And I owe him thanks."

She stared at him, then her eyes misted with tears.

Brogan looked embarrassed. "Rosemarie, how you ever got interested in Seth is beyond me. Such a waste."

She dabbed at her eyes with a kerchief. "I liked Seth. Even after we split, I liked him."

Slocum's face was grim. "Where did you draw against him, Gillis? I thought Seth was traveling with his bunch."

Gillis looked jolted; it was not a question he wanted to answer in front of Rosemarie. You couldn't tell a girl that you had ambushed her ex-sweetie.

Brogan moved in smoothly. "What's the difference how he did it, Slocum? Seth was trying to get me. My boy did the right thing."

Rosemarie threw Gillis a look of contempt, as if aware how he shot Seth. She walked to a nearby boulder, leaned against it, and dried her eyes.

"She'll simmer down," Brogan said to Slocum. "We ought to try to make Honey Creek before dark."

Gillis was scowling. "Such a fuss about Seth, a clunk of

a cowboy. She oughta have more sense."

Brogan shook his head. "Women are funny critters, Gillis. Don't try to understand them."

"I'll talk to her," Slocum said, and he walked to the boulder.

Gillis watched him, his face reddening. "Did you hear him? Trying to clobber me in front of Rosemarie. Where'd you get that sonofabitch?"

Brogan nodded. "Yeah, he had no call to ask you that. He's a foxy dog." He stared hard-eyed at Slocum talking to Rosemarie. "Be careful of him, he's a fast gun. I don't like him. I owe him a couple of hundred, to be paid when we get to Silver Fork, but I've got a gut feelin' he ain't goin' to make it to Silver Fork."

"Be glad to handle it, Dad," Gillis said.

"No. We'll put Mire on him. Dick doesn't care for him either. Just be careful, son. Don't do anything stupid."

"Why do you need him? Seth is out-now."

"What about Seth's bunch? They're his friends. We have to see what they do. They may try to pay you off. You left tracks. They gotta know who shot Seth, unless they're awful stupid. Reckon we'll find out in Honey Creek." He looked thoughtfully at Gillis. "How *did* you shoot Seth?"

"Fired a rifle from high cover."

Brogan's eyes squinted. "You hit him? You're sure?"

Gillis scowled. "'Course I hit him. He went down like a gutshot pig."

Brogan rubbed his chin. "You ain't the world's best shot, Gillis. Did you stick around to make sure?"

Gillis rubbed his nose nervously. "I wish you wouldn't cut me down, Dad. I couldn't stick around. If I fired again, they'd locate me. I had to get out quick. They were goin' to come lookin'."

Brogan nodded. "Reckon you did the right thing, getting out fast. But I wish you had made sure."

Gillis turned to look at Slocum talking to Rosemarie. Their heads were close. He flushed with anger, but he realized the gunfighter was dangerous. You didn't show a man like that that you hated him, not unless you had Mire's gun working for you.

Brogan, too, was disturbed by the way Rosemarie talked to Slocum. Rosemarie was getting mighty interested in that polecat. The best thing to do with Slocum, he thought, was to turn Mire loose on him. Now that Seth was gone, the quicker he got rid of Slocum the better.

"I hate Gillis," Rosemarie was saying to Slocum.

"He's a backshooter," Slocum said.

"I'm so sad about Seth," she said.

He was silent.

"I can't stand to ride with Gillis," she said.

"When we get to Honey Creek, you can drop him there."

"One way or another, we'll drop him there," she agreed.

He stared at her.

"What is it?" she asked.

"How did you get ever involved with the Brogans anyway—a girl like you."

She bit her lip. "Don't ask that now, Slocum. I'll tell you—sometime."

Slocum turned to look at Gillis, and caught his vicious glance. He smiled: that tinpot cowboy was full of bile. He'd have to watch his back.

"Let's ride to Honey Creek," he said.

She wiped her face and they started back to the Brogans.

11

Seth looked west to the gray, massive face of the mountain, then he looked far down the trail; it was level, nothing to be seen.

Seth shook his head sadly; he had to confront the unpleasant fact that Lefty Leon was not coming back. Someone had swallowed him up. Gillis? Not him, he was the sort of gunman who'd shoot himself in the foot. An Apache or Mire? Seth figured out that Lefty, still seething because of the death of his sidekick, Paddy, had searched out Mire for a revenge showdown.

And the worst must have happened. It would be tough to lose Lefty, one of his best guns. That meant Mire had four men to his three. Wouldn't pay to hit the Mire bunch straight on. Seth ground his teeth in frustration. He'd have to come up with something wily. After all, it was Brogan and Gillis that he wanted; Mire just blocked the way, as did Slocum.

Seth felt a streak of melancholy; his luck was lousy, things were sliding downhill. He'd lost his ma, Rosemarie, and now, Lefty. Of course, he still had Fast John and Arne, sturdy fighters, two good guns, but his enemies were powerful. Best not to confront them, especially out here. In town he might even the odds.

He made his way back to the camp; it was pocketed by brush on three sides. John, leaning against a rock, was cleaning his rifle. Seth looked at him with pleasure. Fast John was smiling—his mood was always up, no matter what the odds—he always figured on survival. Arne sat next to him, a taciturn man who never lost his nerve, a strong arm to lean on when the fighting got tough.

They were looking at him.

"I figger Lefty's gone," Seth said.

John shrugged. "Maybe. He might turn up."

Seth shook his head. "I reckon he tried to do it himself, John. That's what went wrong. He's been wanting to get Mire. Probably found the Mire bunch and decided to take them on instead of coming back."

Arne nodded. "That's how I see it. He's chopped down. We've got to move."

"We could reconnoiter, pour gunfire on them from ambush," said John.

"We could, if they were sleeping, but they won't be." Seth waited for Arne, who had a wise head, to say something.

Arne finally spoke. "They have to figger we're around if Lefty barged in on them. And they'll be coming. I think we ought to hightail out of here for Honey Creek. Pick up a couple of gunmen there. Mire has four hot guns. Brogan's got Slocum, he's good. It'd be dumb to meet them out here. They've got the odds."

"Sounds right, Arne," Seth said.

John shrugged. He'd go either way, somehow the odds never bothered him.

Seth sighed. "We'll go for Honey Creek." He moved toward the horses. "Too bad about Lefty."

• • •

Slocum led the way on a trail twisting through land where only a sparse growth of horse chestnut provided tree cover from the sun.

As Brogan rode he started to brood about Rosemarie. He didn't like the way she talked about Seth. He didn't like the way she had moved toward Slocum.

Now, with Seth dead, Brogan felt a surge of power; he'd become the big honcho. Now he owned the Silver Fork— the land, cattle, and horses; now he was one of the richest ranchers in Arizona.

Rosemarie, however, didn't seem to be aware of it. It was time to hit her with it, tell her what he'd done to get her. That damned Slocum was sneaking up on her. True, his gun had saved them from some hellish moments, and women liked the brave warrior, but they also liked the rich, powerful leader—and that was *him*. Brogan was facing the plain fact: he hadn't gotten much of her attention since Slocum had joined them.

Then Slocum, who had dropped back to ride alongside of Rosemarie, glanced behind. He frowned and pulled his roan up short.

"What is it?" demanded Brogan.

"Gillis is ridin' a lame horse," Slocum said.

Brogan glowered. They were not far from Honey Creek and this had to happen. Always Gillis. In a grating voice, he said, "Don't you know when your horse is running lame, Gillis?"

Gillis scowled. "Jest a bit lame. I figgered he could make it to Honey Creek."

Slocum swung off his saddle and looked at the right fore-leg of the lame sorrel. Burrs were buried deep in the hoof. "If you had caught it early, you still could ride her, Gillis, but not now," he said.

Gillis glared. "I still can. Let the bastard limp into Honey Creek."

Slocum smiled. "Gillis, you ain't killin' that horse while I'm riding with you."

Gillis's narrow face flushed red. "Well, mister, you don't hafta ride with us. Seth is dead. We don't need you anymore. As for your money—you can come around Silver Fork in a coupla days and collect it."

Brogan stared at his son, and cursed under his breath. The idea of traveling without a fast gun out here was idiotic. Anything could hit them, Seth's gunmen, drifters, Apaches. Sometimes he wondered how he had sired such a mulehead.

"Who the hell's running this outfit, Gillis?" Brogan growled.

"Well, Dad . . . ," he began.

Brogan put up his hand. "Don't talk. You talk dumb. We'll stop here for a while. Try to dig out the burrs, see if it helps. If it doesn't we'll leave the sorrel."

Gillis went red, consumed with rage and hate. He had been humiliated before Rosemarie by his own father. It was all the fault of Slocum. If only he could pay him back—in triplicate.

He dug into his saddle for his knife, went to the sorrel, lifted the foreleg, and began to pick at the burrs. Brogan came to watch.

Rosemarie sat in the shade on the grass near heavy, tangled brush, leaning on her elbow as she sipped water from her canteen.

Slocum watched Gillis working on the sorrel, then glanced at Rosemarie. "Don't move!" he spoke softly.

They all stared at him as his gun came out in a flash and barked twice. The sidewinder, thick-bodied and poisonous, jumped, writhed, and twisted in agony, then lay still—just inches from Rosemarie. She jumped to her feet, her eyes wide with fear.

"God," she said. "I hate snakes."

Gillis was staring. He was jolted by the blinding speed of Slocum's draw, and the horror of the poisonous snake. It could have killed in a second.

"Holy mother," he muttered.

Brogan was shaken, it had almost been a replay of what had happened to Lottie.

"Wish I had a drink," Brogan said.

Slocum walked over to his saddlebag and pulled out a whiskey bottle.

Brogan grabbed it and took a long gulp.

Slocum poured some in a cup and offered it to Rosemarie. She sipped it. "Thanks, Slocum. Saved my life."

"That like the one who did in Seth's mother, Dad?" Gillis said.

"Same breed." The booze was easing Brogan.

Gillis took the whiskey bottle, drank, and wiped his mouth. "Ain't it funny how they go for the ladies."

Brogan looked slyly at Rosemarie and grinned. "Even in the Bible, the serpent went for Eve first, didn't it? Reckon the snake couldn't sell Adam a bill of goods."

Slocum stared at him. It took a funny mind to think like that, especially when Rosemarie had been a hairbreadth away from an agonizing death.

"You sure shoot a quick gun." Gillis was almost admiring. He hated that Slocum could draw that fast, but realized Rosemarie would be dead otherwise.

"I tole you he was fast," said Brogan. "If I had been fast as you, Slocum, maybe Lottie would be alive today," he said sadly.

Slocum glanced at him, sensing the fake tone of his

voice. "I'll look at the sorrel." He walked to the horse and lifted the foreleg, then he picked up the knife Gillis had dropped and started to dig at the deeply buried burrs.

Gillis came to watch.

Brogan took another pull on the whiskey bottle. He was alone with Rosemarie.

"God, I hate snakes," she said again.

Brogan gazed at her lovely face, her comely figure. "They're not all bad. If not for a snake, we might not be together."

Rosemarie looked at him. She was trying to make up her mind about a lot of things. With Seth dead, Brogan had become sole owner of Silver Fork. That would make him the richest rancher in Arizona. You didn't sneeze that away. He had made it very clear that he was wild about her. She'd seen it from the beginning, the way his eyes burned when he looked at her. At first it had been embarrassing, especially when she and Seth were together.

But she also found it exciting—Brogan, a mature man, in full growth. Compared to him, Seth was a yearling. She respected power in a man. Take Slocum—he'd be ideal, a real lover, a strong protector, but he wouldn't strike roots—men like him didn't, so she was forced back to Brogan.

Brogan, encouraged, took another haul from the bottle. The whiskey made him more daring. "Listen," he said softly. "I've wanted you for a long time, Rosemarie. You know that."

"It's not easy for a woman to know what's in a man's mind."

He stared at her lovely blue eyes, her honey-colored hair, her full figure, and he lusted for her. "You don't know what I went through to get near you," he said.

"Like what?" Her tone was flirtatious.

"It's a secret, but I'm ready to tell you."

That piqued her curiosity, so she waited.

He pointed to where Slocum had killed the snake. "A slimy thing like that was crawling near Lottie. I saw it. All I had to do was pull my gun and shoot it." He paused, his dark eyes burning. "But I didn't, and when she moved, it got her."

Rosemarie listened, fascinated. He had let the snake kill Lottie! That's what he was saying. Why? It shook her. In a way it was—murder.

"I'm telling you this, Rosemarie, because I want you to know how far I'd go for you." His face was grim. "You should keep it in mind. I can see that Slocum appeals to you—an idle flirtation. *But would he do what I've done for you?*"

He smiled. "I'll have the Silver Fork now—the whole ranch. You won't lack for anything. You'll get the best things in life. We can start a dynasty in Arizona." He looked at her. Her eyes were gleaming, but he couldn't read them. He had hit her hard, that was clear. He wouldn't press her now. She needed to digest all that he'd told her, but he had no doubts. Power always dazzled women. Why should she be different?

Brogan felt good.

Now Slocum was coming toward them. "That horse will need a week before it can run again, we'll set him loose. Gillis can ride behind you. Honey Creek ain't that far."

"It's all right, Slocum." Brogan's voice was warm.

Slocum glanced at Rosemarie. She looked like she'd been kicked by a mule. It must have been one helluva talk, Slocum mused, as he swung over his saddle.

Mire looked at his biggest two men, Beyer and Sheehan. "You two take care of Lefty, and say something nice, 'cause he wasn't a bad guy."

Sheehan stood up and glowered at Mire. "Why do you pick on the big men to do the diggin'?"

Mire grinned. "'Cause they need the work most."

Beyer's dark eyes glittered as if amused. He pulled the shovels from the saddles, gave one to Sheehan, and they started digging. After Beyer threw the last shovel of dirt, he muttered, "May the good Lord take care of Lefty. He wasn't a bad guy."

They joined Mire, Lennie, and Allen lazing on slanted rocks. Beyer drank from his canteen and grinned. "Gotta say it, Mire. Lefty sure wanted your hide."

Sheehan smiled. "Lefty was trouble, but he overestimated himself a bit."

"It takes a bit to be very dead," drawled Allen.

Mire turned to his scout, Lennie. "What the hell was he doin' out there when you grabbed him? Aimin' to shoot or what?"

Lennie frowned with remembering. "I got behind him real quiet. He didn't look like he was coming at us. Just scouting. Probably to ride back and tell Seth."

"So what do we do, Mire, wait for Seth or go after him?" asked Sheehan.

Mire rubbed his chin thoughtfully. "They're down to three. Maybe Seth and his boys will come, if we give 'em time."

"Trouble is," drawled Allen, "they might sneak up, try an ambush."

"Yeah, that could happen," said Mire. "You and Beyer do lookout, surprise them."

Allen looked at the gray mountainside. "Ain't much fun hanging around, staring at those crags," he said.

Mire glanced at the sun streaking the sky. "We'll give 'em a piece of time. If they don't come, we'll backtrack Lefty— that should bring us to their camp." He shook his head.

"Too bad they didn't *all* come with Lefty. We'd be through with it."

Beyer and Allen took their rifles and went out for guard duty. Mire started a poker game with the others.

After losing a few dollars, which made him grumpy, Mire stood up and tapped his foot restlessly. A lone eagle soared against the orange-streaked clouds. "Well, we're through here. Let's go after Seth and his two buzzards."

They packed their gear, mounted up, and followed Lennie as he backtracked Lefty's prints.

When they finally located Seth's camp they found it empty.

Lennie studied the ground. "They're headed for Honey Creek."

The men turned to look at Mire.

"That's interesting," he said, grinning. "A saloon's a good place to kill a man. You can always get a drink afterward."

12

The sun blazed from a brassy sky as they rode laboriously toward Honey Creek. The riding was especially tough over the rocky, hilly terrain, which made Slocum glance back at Brogan's weary horse, carrying the double burden.

"Better not press that mare too hard, or we may end up running with only two horses," Slocum said.

Fortunately they found a rivulet where they stopped to let the horses rest and drink. Gillis dropped to the ground, leaning his tired body against a boulder. Brogan sat next to him, drinking from his canteen, then he pulled out a cigar and lit it.

Slocum and Rosemarie walked together downstream, where it was easier to wash and refill their canteens. Slocum pulled off his neckerchief, wet it, and mopped his face. "Sweating like a pig," he said.

"Try not to smell like one," Rosemarie said teasingly.

He flipped water at her and she laughed.

Gillis, watching them with his washed-out blue eyes, jerked his thumb. "Look how that hombre makes up to Rosemarie. Why do you let him, Dad?"

Brogan looked, and his eyes glinted viciously. "Let him? He's a fast gun, I tole you. And I'm telling you again." He puffed on his cigar. "I don't like it either, Gillis, but

I don't take it seriously. They're just talkin', it don't mean anything."

"I don't like that hombre," said Gillis. "Maybe I'll put a bullet in his back—we'd save a coupla hundred."

Brogan looked at him sternly. "Don't try it—you'll die. You hear me?"

Gillis squirmed. "I hear you."

Brogan's jaw set hard. "Don't fret about Slocum. He'll get it when the time's right." He smiled brightly. "As for Rosemarie, you can figger she's goin' to be your new ma. You like that, boy?"

Gillis grinned broadly. "Yeah, it'd be nice to have a looker like her in the family."

Slocum, drinking from his canteen, glanced back and caught Brogan and Gillis looking at him. He picked up their malice and grinned. "There's more venom in those two gents than in the reptile I just shot."

Rosemarie looked startled. "Why'd you say that?"

He laughed. "You gotta be blind not to see that Brogan craves you as much as he craves the ranch. As for Gillis, I've seen vultures look at me with the same expression."

She laughed. "Oh, Gillis is bad. But don't underestimate Brogan."

"Hard to do that." Slocum gazed at her. "What in hell was he talking about after I shot the snake? He looked like he was in a stew."

She turned away as if trying to wipe something out of her mind, then said, "That's what he talked about, the snake."

"Must have been rough," he said. "You looked like you'd been kicked by a mule."

She brushed back her hair, thinking hard. "Slocum, I owe you a lot. You keep saving my life. You ought to be mighty careful about Brogan. He thinks I like you too much. And he's dangerous."

"How dangerous?"

"Plenty." She paused. "That snake—you saw it and shot it. Brogan had a chance to kill the snake before it killed Lottie." She paused. "But he didn't."

Slocum was silent.

She went on. "He said he did it for me, to get *rid* of her. He wanted me and she was in the way. That's what he said—to prove how much he cared. He wants to marry me." She looked away. "Imagine me, *stepmother* to Gillis. Imagine Brogan making love to me. And me thinking about him waiting and watching for the snake to bite Lottie. Now I can't stand the sight of Brogan. But I'm afraid."

Slocum smiled grimly. From the beginning there'd been a bad smell about Brogan. He'd been phony, passing Rosemarie off as his niece, now he was phony about Seth. Seth had been right all along. This lowlife, Brogan, had murdered his mother for the ranch and for Rosemarie. Seth wasn't a loco cowboy, after all, he knew who his enemies were.

Slocum considered the angles. "Well," he said, "that sure changes things. It's a pity Seth is dead." He gazed at her. "If I were you, I'd not give Brogan the idea that you think he's lower than a snake's belly. He's not a nice fella."

She looked solemn, but said nothing.

He looked at her. "Are you sure you want to give up the Silver Fork? Maybe you'd like being a rich lady."

"Well," she said slowly, "to tell the truth, until Brogan told me about Lottie, I did like the idea." She studied him. "The Brogans are tricky polecats; I worry about you." She glanced back at Brogan now calmly smoking, looking at the mountains to the west. "Remember Mire. He works for Brogan. They say he's one of the great gunfighters of Tombstone. Faster than Doc Holliday."

Slocum shrugged. "They're always saying stuff. I know about Doc Holliday. Lots of legends are hot air. I've known fast guns who had no reps at all, and lucky shooters with big reps. I'm not saying Mire ain't fast. He's fast enough."

Slocum stood up and looked at the sky. "Well, let's go to Honey Creek, and see if things can sort themselves out."

When they reached the Brogans, Gillis gave Slocum a yellow smile. Slocum almost laughed: he'd seen a smile like that on a crocodile.

When they started to ride, Slocum took the rear position. He knew a backshooter when he saw one, and Gillis looked like an ace backshooter.

Mire was standing against a jutting rock, looking down in the valley, when he saw the stagecoach running toward them.

They watched it closely. It had four guards, two in front, two behind.

"That would be the stage out of Tucson," said Lennie.

"What are you thinking, Mire?" Sheehan asked.

Mire's eyes were glittering. "About the cargo."

"Right, it's gotta be gold," said Allen.

"Yeah, and carrying guards, each a crackerjack gun," said Lennie.

"And what the hell are we, gooney birds?" asked Beyer.

"For the sake of argument," said Sheehan, "suppose someone wanted to hit that stage, how'd he do it?"

Mire studied the land, then pointed. "Well, if I wanted to, I'd plant my men on that pass a mile ahead. It's rocky, narrow, and they've got to go through it. They'd get a helluva surprise."

"And we'd get bags of gold," said Allen.

"Interesting to think about," said Mire.

"You've got about eight minutes to think." Lennie smiled.

Mire reflected. "Our job is to knock off Seth and his boys. Though I'm a low-down coyote, I like to keep my word."

"Why can't we knock off the stage, and still knock off Seth and his boys?" Allen grinned cheerfully.

"You've got five minutes," drawled Sheehan. "After that, they could spot us, and we'll lose the surprise."

"Let's do it," said Mire.

They slipped back, out of sight of the stage, took to their horses and raced north along a zigzag trail through scattered brush and juniper. They climbed over jutting rocks and positioned themselves on the shelf of the pass. They lay flat and waited, rifles in hand.

The stagecoach climbed up the twisting slope and the horses strained until they reached the approach to the pass.

Mire peered out from his position and watched the straining horses pick up speed as they started downhill. The driver looked carefree as he talked to his partner riding shotgun on the front seat.

He cracked his whip over the running horses. In the rear position the two guards looked curiously at the steep rocks but saw nothing suspicious.

As the stage rocketed through the pass, Mire and his bunch unleashed a fusillade of gunfire. The driver and his front-seat companion never knew what hit them. The two rear guards got their rifles up, but the barrage of bullets knocked them flat, and they went down like tinder in a tornado.

Mire and his men climbed down to view the carnage.

The stage men lay torn and bleeding.

"A bloody day," said Allen, running his hand through his curly hair.

"Riding stage is dangerous work," said Mire.

"What the hell, it's a short life," said Beyer.

"Let's get the money," said Sheehan.

Inside the coach they found a small, iron safe with a huge steel lock. It looked impregnable. They went through the pockets of the dead men but found no keys. They dragged the safe out and stared at it. They shot at it, picked at it, and kicked it, but they couldn't crack it.

They sat around in frustration and stared.

"Did we kill a lot of men for nothing?" asked Allen.

"What the hell do we do?" asked Beyer, his mouth wrenched in anger.

Mire had made up his mind. "I'll tell you what we'll do. We'll bury that safe and leave it here 'til we come back with dynamite. And that will be *after* we do what we were hired to do."

Beyer stared at him. "I don't like that, Mire."

Mire's jaw hardened. "Why so, Beyer?"

Beyer stroked his chin, his pale, gray eyes gleaming with mistrust. He was a powerfully-built man with a record of five kills in Tombstone. "For one thing, someone might find it, go off with it."

"Doubt that," Mire spoke calmly.

Beyer studied the faces around him. "How do we know one of us might not come back on the sly, dynamite it, and take off?"

"Gotta have a little faith," said Sheehan.

"I lost faith years ago," said Beyer.

Mire considered. "If we stick together, that won't happen."

Beyer persisted. "We're goin' into town. There'll be showdowns. Anything could happen. What I say is, gold in the hand is worth two in the ground." He looked around. "Anyone agree?"

There was silence.

"I still don't like it," said Beyer.

Then Mire moved back. "Pull your gun, Beyer."

Beyer felt a chill and stared. "Did I hear you right?"

"You heard me," Mire drawled.

Beyer stared at Mire's icy gaze. "Why?"

"I figger anyone who thinks like you might be too greedy. Gotta keep this bunch clean. So draw your gun."

Beyer turned pale. "Hell, Mire, I was just talkin'. I'll stick with your decision."

"You spoke your piece. Too late to believe you, Beyer. Now, draw."

"Ain't goin' to pull my gun. It's murder."

Mire's voice went icy. "This is the last time. Draw."

Beyer went for his gun before Mire spoke the last word, but it was hopeless. His gun got out of the holster and he fell with a bullet in his chest. He staggered, twisted, and fell on his back. His gray eyes, in a fury, stayed on Mire as he died.

Mire glanced at the others. "We're all for one and one for all. Now let's bury the safe and go to Honey Creek."

For a time, Mire and his bunch rode silently through gaunt, rugged land, past saw-toothed crags. The sky had softened with rosy-hued clouds. Mire figured they couldn't be more than five miles from Honey Creek. The trail climbed, and Lennie, first to reach the crest, looked down on the plains and saw the four riders following the twisting stretch of trail.

"Well," he said, "lookit down there. It's Brogan and Gillis on one horse traveling toward Honey Creek."

The men all looked, then Mire smiled. "And that's the bonny filly with them. Rosemarie, girl of our dreams."

The men laughed.

"Who's the gent?" asked Sheehan.

"That's Slocum. He saved Brogan's hide near Tucson. Brogan thinks he's a fast gun." He stared down. "What the hell's Gillis doin' down there?"

Slocum had sighted them and spoke to Brogan who turned and waved. They dismounted and waited for Mire and his bunch to come riding up fast. The men swung off their horses, looked at Rosemarie and smiled, then examined Slocum curiously.

"Horse trouble?" Mire asked.

"Gillis," Brogan said. "His sorrel went lame. What about you? Any trouble?"

Mire smiled as he thought of the stage. Why talk about that? He'd talk about Lefty.

"No real trouble," he said. "We picked up Lefty Leon, one of Seth's boys. He was snoopin', we took care of him." He smiled broadly at Rosemarie. "Nice to see a good-looking woman." He jerked his thumb at his men. "'Specially after looking at those mugs all day." He threw an acid eye at Gillis, "Surprised to see Gillis with you. Expected he'd be at the ranch, keepin' an eye on things. Seth might ride in; you never know."

At mention of Seth, Brogan stiffened. Both Slocum and Rosemarie turned to look at Mire.

"Did I say something peculiar?" Mire asked.

"Seth's dead," Brogan said. "Gillis shot him."

There was a moment of silence, then the men laughed. Mire glanced at Gillis but said nothing.

Brogan felt his nerves tighten. "What's so funny?" He watched Mire take out a cigar and light it.

"I'll tell you what's funny," Mire drawled. "Seems that back a piece, Gillis took a shot at Seth. Though the bullet missed him, Seth didn't like it, so he sent Lefty Leon to find out and take care of who did it." Mire pulled on his cigar. "Lefty started after Gillis, but stopped when he picked up our trail. We saw the signs later. Seems Lefty was more interested in paying me off for shooting Paddy Tavish." Mire looked casually at Gillis. "Poor Lefty, in the shoot-out he came in second best. I reckon it gave Gillis more breathin' time."

Brogan thought about what he'd just heard, then his eyes blazed, and stepping close, he slapped Gillis.

Gillis grabbed his cheek. "What'd you do that for?" he whined.

Brogan glared. "You come to me tellin' how you shot Seth, but you never stayed to find out. Always braggin'. You'd be pushin' daisies now, if not for Mire here, 'cause Lefty woulda shot your ass off."

Slocum stroked his chin, thinking that Gillis didn't seem to do anything right. The fact that Seth was alive, however, made Slocum thoughtful, but he wasn't surprised. It was hard to believe that Gillis, even from ambush, could successfully shoot Seth. Slocum unloosened his neckerchief and wiped his face. Things looked different with Seth alive. His sympathies were strongly for that cowboy who had lost his mother, his girl, and his ranch, and was trying valiantly to fight back. There were three men with Mire, there had been four; he remembered seeing them ride in through the window in the Locust Grove café. One had dropped by the wayside; he wondered how.

"I'm glad Seth is alive," Rosemarie said softly.

Brogan's grin was malignant. "It's temporary, Rosemarie. Think of him as dead."

Mire's glance at Rosemarie was curious. "Thought you were through with Seth."

She frowned. "I don't want him dead."

Mire shrugged. "Everyone dies."

Brogan shook his head. "We're not in a hurry. We've got some fine livin' to do." He grinned at Rosemarie.

Mire walked closer to Brogan. "You're movin' slow, minus a horse. Why don't we ride ahead? Get to town and look around."

"I'll go along," said Slocum.

Brogan looked surprised. "I thought you were ridin' all the way with me?"

"You've got Gillis. You don't need me. I've got some things to do."

Brogan's eyes narrowed. Slocum could see that he didn't like it, but he didn't care. Rosemarie was frowning, but that could wait, too. Slocum had some things in mind.

Mire spoke to Allen. "You stay with Brogan." He mounted up and turned to Slocum. "No reason why you can't ride with us. I remember you saved my hide back in Locust Grove." He turned to his men. "Some joker wanted to shoot my ass and Slocum stepped in to help." He waved at Rosemarie. "See you in Honey Creek."

The horses pounded the earth as Mire and Slocum rode out in front of the men.

Brogan watched them. He had nasty forebodings about Slocum; something was biting that cowboy's ass. What? He was a dangerous gun and Brogan felt nervous about him. That polecat had to be taken care of, the sooner the better.

Rosemarie, too, watched Slocum as he rode tall in the saddle. She didn't like it. She liked his presence, she liked to have him near; she felt safer. She was surprised that he left her with Brogan, especially after she had told him of her feelings. She bit her lip, feeling anger at Slocum.

Then she started thinking about Seth.

13

If Bill McCabe, sheriff of Honey Creek, had his way, he'd keep the town quiet and lawful. And he could do it, he was fast and had three strong deputies. The sheriff was sturdy, broad-shouldered, and popular with the townsfolk, but he was also a practical man who understood the ways of cowboys. They rode the range in all weather, a boring and lonely life, so when they came to town they liked a lively time, and that meant liquor, ladies, and gambling. The town needed the spending, and the sheriff bent over backward to let the boys have their fun, but cowboys who carried guns and gulped whiskey tended to get touchy and quarrelsome. There'd been too many fist- and gunfights after sundown. The shop owners complained and the killings were bad for business and the town's reputation, so Sheriff McCabe put a tight rein on gunfights in Honey Creek.

When Seth and his gunfighters rode into town, Sheriff McCabe's brow furrowed. He knew Arne and Fast John, men with reps in the Arizona Territory, but they were not obstreperous. They went quietly into the saloon, and when he dropped in for a look an hour later, they seemed calm enough, drinking at their table. But it wasn't yet sundown, the liquor wasn't flowing, and the ladies weren't flirting.

At sundown, however, when the sheriff, picking his teeth

outside his office, noted Mire riding into town, he didn't like the feeling. Riding alongside of Mire was a lean, powerful hombre who looked dangerous. He didn't know that gent, but he did know the other two tough gunfighters, Sheehan and Lennie.

Sheriff McCabe headed them off in the middle of the dirt street. Mire and the riders behind him pulled their horses and the dust of the street swirled.

The sheriff's blue eyes were cool. "Howdy, Mire. Passin' through?"

Mire nodded pleasantly. "Might stop for a bite and a drink, sheriff."

Sheriff McCabe studied the four tough-looking riders. Fast guns, he was thinking, every blasted one. "Let's keep the peace, Mire."

Mire looked injured. "I'm a peaceful man, sheriff."

"Yeah—so how come there's always hombres dyin' around you?"

Mire grinned broadly. "Can't help it, sheriff, if some boys with a snootful of whiskey get uppity and try to beat my draw."

Sheriff McCabe's blue eyes glowed. "You don't have to take the challenge, Mire. The saloon always gets bloody when you're in town." He looked respectfully at the lean, powerful green-eyed cowboy. "Who's this gent?"

"This is John Slocum," Mire said.

"A man of peace," Slocum said.

The sheriff nodded. "Let's hope so. Boothill in Honey Creek is runnin' outa burial space. That's not what I get paid for."

He looked at them, then swung his keen gaze at Sheehan and Lennie. "Mind you boys keep the peace."

As they rode past him, Mire frowned. "Best not go to

the saloon and start the blood flowing. We do it later, when things heat up. In the excitement, at the right time, we can do plenty of damage." He looked down the street at the sign of the Lonely Cowboy's Café. "Let's get some decent grub."

They rode to the café, where Slocum, looking through the window, didn't see who he was looking for.

As Mire swung off his horse, Slocum said, "Reckon I'm more thirsty than hungry. I'll see you boys later." Without waiting, he wheeled the roan and started back toward the saloon.

Mire watched him with a scowl. "That hombre worries me."

"Worries me, too," said Sheehan. "You don't know what he's thinkin'. You say he's fast."

"I never saw him. Brogan says it."

Sheehan shrugged. "How would Brogan know a fast gun?"

Mire smiled. "He might. He hired me."

They went into the café.

Slocum pushed open the swinging doors. It was a spacious saloon, with a long bar, a square mirror behind it, and five gambling tables with players. Several saloon ladies in sleek, tight dresses sat at tables with customers. Slocum recognized two men at the bar, Seth's gunfighters, with whiskey glasses in front of them. They were husky polecats, and they were watching him closely.

He sauntered to the bar, took a position next to them and smiled. "I'm Slocum."

"We know it," said the dark-eyed, big-bellied one who would be Fast John. The other man would be Arne; an honest face, Slocum thought.

"I'm here on a peace mission," Slocum said.

"That so?"

They glanced at the doors, as if expecting other gunmen in the Mire bunch would show.

"How come your friend, Mire, isn't with you?" asked Arne.

"He's no friend," said Slocum, his green eyes hard.

"Where is he?"

"Eating dinner at the café."

The barman came up and looked curiously at Slocum.

"Whiskey," Slocum said.

Slocum drank, then glanced at the back table where Seth was sitting alone, watching them.

"I'd like to talk to Seth," Slocum said, looking over at the table.

"Why?" John asked.

Slocum smiled. "I'd like to tell him some things he'd like to hear."

Arne studied Slocum for a while. "Just hold it." He walked over to Seth, spoke to him, then came back and jerked his finger toward Seth.

When he reached the table, Seth motioned to the chair. "Sit down."

They looked at each other. Slocum noted the porkpie hat he favored, his clear eyes in a strong young face. "What's on your mind, Slocum?"

"I've been traveling with Brogan and Rosemarie."

Seth's face was stony. "I know it. So what?"

"Learned a few things."

Seth showed sudden interest. "Like what?"

"Like things you told me are true."

Seth's face hardened. "What things?"

"Brogan is greedy and after everything you've got."

"You found that out? That ain't much." Seth lifted his whiskey glass.

"No, but it took time to find out. Gillis thought he shot you."

Seth's face twisted. "Gillis couldn't hit the side of a barn."

"He told Brogan that he shot you. Brogan thought he had the ranch, and told Rosemarie that he'd done plenty to get her."

Seth's face was a cold study. "What'd he do?"

Slocum hitched his gunbelt, glanced at the door, then looked straight at Seth. "That snake story. You almost guessed it. Brogan had a chance to shoot the damned sidewinder, but he didn't."

There was a long silence. Seth's face whitened with rage. "It's like I thought—he's a vicious dog. He'll pay. If I do nothing else in this world, I'll make him pay." He stared at Slocum. "Why have you come to tell me?"

"I'da been here before, but thought they wiped you out. Then I heard you were okay."

A suspicious gleam came to Seth's eyes. "How'd you hear that?"

"Mire and his bunch caught up with us. He told us about Lefty."

Seth looked grieved. Just as he figured, Lefty had gone after Mire instead of Gillis. "So Mire shot Lefty?"

Slocum nodded.

"Mire is deadly," Seth said, looking depressed. "He can't be beat. But I'm goin' after Brogan and Gillis; I've got to get them before Mire gets here."

Slocum smiled. The hombre had guts. "Those two men at the bar, is that all you've got?"

Seth nodded. "That's it. Ain't nobody here is goin' to line up against Mire."

"Well, you can count on my gun, if you want it," Slocum said.

Seth was caught by surprise. Why would Slocum swing to him? Was it one of Brogan's tricks? Seth remembered Slocum saying back in the Locust Grove saloon that he had really put his gun behind Rosemarie, not Brogan, but he had learned what a vulture Brogan was. Seth felt a rush of feeling. This lean, strong man with the green eyes in front of him was a straight shooter, he felt it. "If you mean that, Slocum, I'm right proud to have you with us."

"I'm glad to help. Thought I'd mention that Mire and a couple of his men are in town. The sheriff has put out a warning about shootings."

Just then the door opened and Sheehan came in with Lennie. "Just had a lousy grub at the local café," Sheehan said loudly. "Not much of a town."

They swaggered to the bar where Sheehan spotted Fast John and Arne drinking. He studied them. Fast John was potbellied, yet they called him fast—a mystery. Arne had a rugged face and a body built for speed; Sheehan suspected he'd be the dangerous one. What did it matter? They had to go through these two polecats to get to Seth.

The barman was very busy down at the other end. While Sheehan waited, he stroked his chin and did some hard thinking. Mire had hired him back in Tombstone because he was a fast gun. In his early days Sheehan had started out as a cowpuncher. One night, playing faro, he got into a ruckus with a whiskey-soaked hombre. Words exploded and the hombre told Sheehan to pull his gun. Sheehan was young, he'd never shot anyone and his nerves tightened. The drunk sneered and said if Sheehan didn't pull his gun, he'd get shot full of daylight. Sheehan gritted his teeth, took the crouch, and jerked his gun. To his amazement he beat the drunk, his challenger's gun hadn't even cleared the holster. That was Sheehan's baptism of fire. He wondered if he was fast. The next time a cocky gunman pushed him in Fort Smith, he took the challenge, and again, in the showdown, beat his opponent easily. He suspected that he had a fast draw and, after that, his gunfights converted his suspicion into belief.

In Tombstone, Mire had seen him in a fight against one of the Clantons. "Come join us, Sheehan," Mire said afterward. "The work will be interesting and the money good." Sheehan knew of Mire; everyone in Tombstone knew that he had a lightning draw, and had put a lot of customers into Boothill.

"It'd be a pleasure to work for you," said Sheehan. Then Mire told him it was for Brogan, a rancher down in Maricopa who was on the verge of becoming rich. "When that happens," Mire said, "we'll get an extra bonus."

That's what had brought Sheehan into the saloon in Honey Creek, facing these two hombres in Seth's bunch.

They had to go through these hombres to get to Seth, but there was no hurry. Mire had gone for a haircut and told him and Lennie, "Don't do anything unless you've got a good setup. Leave Seth for me. It's gotta be right, otherwise we run into sheriff trouble."

Sheehan waved his hand at the barman who had worked his way toward them. "Hey, good fella, how about a bit of your best."

The barman grinned and poured the whiskey. "That'll be two bits."

Lennie tasted the whiskey. "Overpriced."

Sheehan swilled his glass as if it was a thimble. "Didn't feel it, but I tasted it."

The barman poured two more and stood there.

Sheehan looked at him. "What's the handle?"

"Bill Casey."

"One of the brethren. You oughta know good whiskey.

How come you're selling this rotgut?"

"Best rotgut in the territory." Casey grinned. "You don't like our food, don't like our liquor, don't like our town."

"Mebbe you oughta keep on ridin'," sneered one of the drinkers, a beefy, red-haired cowboy.

Sheehan looked mean-eyed. "I shot a man who looked like you once, but maybe I didn't kill him. Do I have to try again?"

The beefy cowboy paled. There was something sudden and dangerous about this gunfighter.

"I'm sorry," he said. "No offense."

Sheehan smiled, then ignored him. He talked to the barman. "Don't like your sheriff, either. If I had my way, we woulda bypassed this town."

Lennie looked around the saloon and saw the women. "They've got nice tarts here," he said.

"We ain't here for tarts," Sheehan said, lifting his glass.

Lennie continued his scrutiny and stared when he saw Slocum sitting with Seth. He turned to Sheehan. "I do believe Mr. Slocum is consortin' with the enemy."

Sheehan grinned malevolently. "Mr. Slocum is playing a two-faced game."

"What do we do about that?" Lennie asked.

Sheehan lowered his voice, "First things first." He nodded his head at Fast John. "Reckon we'll have to go through these gents to get to Seth."

"What about Slocum? Is he with us or agin us?"

"Leave it to Mire. We'll find out soon enough," Sheehan said, pouring another drink and downing it. Casey was standing nearby, watching him, amused. Sheehan looked at him. "My gut goes into shock every time your whiskey hits it, Casey."

It didn't faze Casey. "You're just drinkin' it today. I drink it all year. Don't expect sympathy."

Lennie leaned forward and raised his voice. "Casey ain't particular about his whiskey, and he ain't particular about *who* he serves."

The remark was picked up by the men nearby and their voices became subdued.

Fast John turned to Arne. "Did you hear some loudmouth criticizing the whiskey?"

Arne smiled. "I heard him. But I see him packin' it away quicker'n anyone else."

Sheehan's pink face went pinker. He turned to face them. "They call you *Fast* John. That right?"

"Right," said John, his eyes a bit fiery, recognizing the opening gambit.

Sheehan glanced at the onlookers. "I knew an hombre in Waco they called *Fast* Eddie. Called him that because he had the slowest gun in town."

There was a small titter from the spectators, then the silence became heavy as the men watched. The silence spread to other parts of the saloon.

"I suppose that's funny," said John, turning. "You're Sheehan. I've heard of you. You got a big rep."

Sheehan grinned. "I deserve it. What do they say?"

"That you got a big rep from pickin' on slow shooters."

The cowboys drinking nearby edged away, aware that something unpleasant could suddenly happen.

Sheehan's big face crumbled into a grin. "John, I figger I've just been insulted, and I'm sorry to tell you this, but I put eleven men in Boothill for remarks even *less* insultin'."

"Hey, Sheehan," said Lennie, "I thought it was *ten* men."

"Eleven—counting Fast John," said Sheehan, and his gun move was a blur. There was a shattering roar of gunfire; both men staggered and fell, hitting the floor. Sheehan brought his hand to his chest, looked at the blood. He coughed, then managed to laugh. "You sonofabitch, you spoiled my rep."

Fast John grinned. "Meetcha in hell, Sheehan." He shut his eyes.

One of the gray-bearded old-timers stared. "Man and boy, I've seen gunfights in Arizona and Texas, but never a fight like this. A dead heat. Both fast as lightnin'. This is for the history books, Charlie."

Charlie, another old-timer standing next to him, had a wary eye on Lennie. "This fracas may not be over yet," he whispered.

"Don't think the sheriff's goin' to like it," another man said. "He's been tryin' to tone down the shootings."

Charlie took off his hat and scratched his head. "Glad I seen this one. To tell my grandson."

14

Lennie stared down at Sheehan. He'd seen Sheehan knock off some very tough gunfighters. Sheehan had ten notches on his gun, yet there he was, dead on the saloon floor. Did he slow down or did he underestimate Fast John? Lennie glanced at Arne, and wondered if this one, too, would be a quick gun. Lennie was worried—he was alone, while they had not only Arne, but Seth and Slocum, who was chancy—Lennie didn't know where Slocum had put his gun. Lennie felt a quiver of fear and decided he'd not do anything, just wait for Mire. Mire was, after all, the "Invincible Gun."

Arne was staring at him, waiting for him to make a move, but Lennie smiled. "I'd call it a tie. They were both fast."

Seth had come forward and was scowling. He liked Fast John, and sorrowed at his death, even though he had taken out Sheehan, one of Mire's fastest guns; losing John was costly.

"They were both fast," Arne said, grim-faced. "But it doesn't pay to be just as fast, you hafta be faster."

The doors swung open and Sheriff McCabe, who'd heard the shooting, came in with two deputies. He looked grimly at the dead men.

The doors opened again and Mire stood there, hard-faced. He, too, had heard the shooting.

The sheriff glowered at the barman.

"They drew on each other," Casey said. "It was a dead tie."

The sheriff motioned to a couple of men who carried the bodies out. He watched them, then stared at Seth, Lennie, Slocum, and Mire.

"This town is getting a rep for killings," he drawled. "That rep is bad for business. We don't like it." He stroked his heavy chin. "If anyone here's got a grievance, he better take it somewhere else, outa town." His smile was ironical. "We're running outa space in Boothill."

He turned to Mire. "There's goin' to be no more show-downs here tonight, Mire."

"If you say so, sheriff. I'm a law-abidin' citizen."

Lennie had to hide a grin. He was thinking of the stage-coach, and the buried safe. Law-abiding!

Mire looked at Slocum standing near Seth, and his eyes narrowed. He stepped to the bar. "Whiskey. I'm dyin' of thirst."

Mire studied Slocum. "Lemme buy you a drink."

"Why not?" Slocum was genial. "And I'll buy you one, Seth."

Mire smiled slowly. "Sure, whyn't you join us, Seth?"

Seth looked at Arne, who stepped close to him.

Mire saw it and shrugged. "We've got a truce."

He drank his whiskey, then wiped his mouth. "We got our differences, but we don't have to settle them now. "He smiled balefully. "There's always time for dyin'."

Slocum lifted his glass. "Yeah—there's always time for dying."

Sheriff McCabe and his deputies took a seat at a front

table, which gave them a broad view of the bar.

Mire shook his head. "Seth, I've got to hand it to you. Didn't think you had a gunslick who could measure up to Sheehan."

"Lost a good man in Fast John," Seth said sorrowfully.

Mire's face was hard. "You gotta think like this—good men don't lose."

Seth drank and began to follow his own thoughts. "Hey, Mire, I want to ask you something. How'd you get mixed up with Brogan? That coyote is as crooked as a dog's leg."

Mire laughed. "Tell you the truth, I like Brogan. He's crooked—but honest crooked. Lots of folks are secret crooked."

Seth grimaced. "And he's paying you plenty."

"He's paying."

"S'pose I pay you more? Would you come over?"

Mire shook his head. "Can't do that. I can't turn on my hire. It'd ruin my rep."

"Doesn't it bother you that Brogan's tryin' to steal my ranch?"

Mire shrugged. "You never know who's right. He thinks you're trying to kill him 'cause of your ma."

Seth gritted his teeth. "He deserves killin' because of that."

Mire grinned. "If all the men who deserved killin' got killed, we wouldn't have space to bury 'em." He turned to stare at Slocum. "You been mighty quiet."

Slocum lifted his drink. "I been thinking what a pure-blooded buzzard you are, Mire."

Mire grinned fiendishly. "Wouldn't have it any other way. And you? You threw in with Brogan, too. You ain't so clean."

"Didn't know what a skunk he was."

Mire's lip curled. "He bought you for a couple of hundred. Just cut the bullshit, Slocum."

Slocum's green eyes were piercing. "That's not how it happened. But now that I know Brogan, I ain't on his side."

"Are you on the side or are you against him?" Mire's voice was icy.

There was a long pause. Seth anxiously watched Slocum.

"Against him."

Mire laughed. "Well, Slocum, this is a free country. Just hope you don't *live* to regret your decision."

"I've got into the habit of living, Mire, and I like it," Slocum said, lifting his drink.

Mire shrugged. "Well, tonight there's a truce. Another day maybe all hell will break loose." He stood up and stretched.

"Where you headed?" asked Slocum.

"Who knows? Brogan's due in town." He glanced at Seth. "With a friend of yours—Rosemarie. I've got nuthin' to do. When the time comes, I'll figger out what to do." He glanced at Lennie. "You stay put. I'm goin' out." Mire wasn't about to tell Lennie that he was going to buy dynamite to eventually blast open the buried safe. How could he know if Lennie would still be nearby when it came to a divvy of the buried money? He sauntered to the doors, pushed them apart, and went out.

"So Rosemarie is ridin' in?" Seth looked strained.

Slocum smiled. "She seemed real happy to discover you weren't dead. You like the girl, right?"

Seth's voice was bitter. "Does it make any difference?" He walked back to his table and poured himself a drink.

Sheriff McCabe glanced around. "Things look nice and quiet. Let's hope it stays that way." He went out the door, followed by his deputies.

Slocum leaned on the bar and thought about Mire. Mire was a quick gun, damned quick. Back in the café he sure pulled his gun fast to shoot down the poor hombre who'd been tracking him. Slocum had heard someone call Mire the "Invincible Gun." Slocum meditated about that; he'd met a lot of Invincible Guns. After you had the luck to beat a few men, you lost your humility and believed you couldn't be beat. That's when you caught the final bullet. Slocum tried never to lose his humility. Somebody out there could be a hairbreadth faster. Sometimes it paid to worry a bit—and work to get the edge.

"I'm thirsty, mister. Will you buy a girl a drink?" She looked a bit tight. She was young and comely, with a button nose, full lips, clear, satiny skin, and a nice figure.

"Give the lady a drink," Slocum said to Casey.

"Annabelle is the name," she said.

"A nice name."

"I'm a nice girl." She drank, then said, "You look like a man in the mood for fun."

Slocum looked grim. It seemed a good idea to get your fun while you could; you never knew when that final bullet might be coming at you. He looked at her and smiled. She seemed still unspoiled, able to enjoy sex. He felt horny and decided it wouldn't hurt to ease the torments of the flesh with sweet Annabelle.

With the intuition of a woman, she read his inclinations. "Come into my parlor," she said, starting for the stairs.

He followed her, and enjoyed the cut of her butt as she moved. From the balcony, he looked down on the players at the card games, and at Seth sitting gloomily with Arne at the table.

The room was cosy, with a window that gazed out on the main street and its stores; beyond were the mountains that towered against a flame-streaked sky.

When he turned, she was already sprawled on the bed, nude as a jaybird. Her breasts were round and hefty. Her tummy was flat, her legs well-rounded, and between her thighs was a crest of curly hair.

He sighed. She was deliciously designed for pleasure, and so young. He stepped out of his Levi's and she looked at him and smiled. "Nothing's as interesting to a woman as the sight of a man's excitement."

His mouth went for one erect nipple and her hands began stroking him.

After a time of this, her eyes glittered. She threw him a sullen look, dropped between his knees, pressed her face against him, and in a surge of excitement, began a frenzy of movement with her mouth. It went on and on, and he yielded to the sheer pleasure. She stopped and looked at the way he was pulsating. "That could give a woman a lot of pleasure," she said. "You know what I'd like," she drawled. "For you to treat me like a bitch, really do me like a stallion that ain't had sex for a month."

He scowled. Well, he'd try to oblige the lady. He crawled over her, grabbed her body and didn't waste a moment. He slipped quickly past the fuzzy mat to the warmth within, thrusting firmly so that he went all the way, and heard her sharp intake of breath. He was large, and she was nice and tight against his flesh; she felt it, too, for she began to squirm and groan. He started slow, moved faster, then grabbed her silky butt with strong hands, thrusting hard against her. He could hear her sharp gasps, little squeals and groans. It was hard to tell whether it was pain or pleasure, but he didn't stop. Her fingers gripped his back, her nails cut his flesh. He thrust violently until he felt the big surge. She twisted from side to side, groaning through clenched teeth.

He lay still for a while, then looked down at her flushed face, expecting to see an outraged tigress, but her face was glowing with pleasure. When it comes to sex, he thought, you can't match the woman. You think you're roughing them, but instead, you're booting them to paradise.

Seth, sitting at the table with Arne, was drinking and thinking about how much he hated Brogan. He had hated him almost at first sight, sensing his trickery. It was funny, Seth thought, that women didn't seem to pick up on the evil in men. Especially lonely women.

It was now four years since his mother lost his father. Seth had marvelous memories of his father: A red-blooded honcho who enjoyed his life, a real man; he'd fought the Apaches in the early years. And with the sweat of his brow and sweat of his mind, buying and selling smart, he had built a huge ranch stocked with great herds of cattle and horses.

Then one cursed day, when his father had been riding the stage from Phoenix, the Apaches attacked. Everyone in the stagecoach was slaughtered. His father sold his life dearly. The Apaches, respecting bravery, did not mutilate his body.

The death of his father was something Seth could hardly get over. His mother mourned deeply and seemed inconsolable. She was a warm-blooded woman who loved and needed the love of a man. But few men could step into the shoes of someone like his father. Then along came Brogan who was prepossessing and cunning. From the beginning Seth sensed he was fake. He tried to warn his mother, but how could you tell a woman, lonely for male companionship, whose flesh still yearned for a man's caresses, that her suitor was a con man. She laughed off his warnings as the natural jealousy of a son.

After the marriage, when that greedy coyote fastened his eyes on Rosemarie, Brogan's character became clearer to

Seth. Brogan was a faithless dog who had married for money, who craved a younger woman, and who managed to bring about the death of his mother.

If ever there was a coyote rotten through and through, it was Brogan! Seth ground his teeth, remembering. To complete his unspeakable evil, he conspired with his mulish son, Gillis, to try and wipe him out. This con man, Brogan, who came out of nowhere, who started with nothing, had destroyed his mother, stolen his girl, and was now, finally, trying to steal his ranch. He deserved merciless killing.

Seth stood up abruptly. "I've got to get out, Arne."

Arne stared. "What's the matter?"

"I need some fresh air."

"I'll come with you."

"No. Stay here. Keep an eye on that one." He pointed to Lennie who had drifted to a card table.

Seth went out of the saloon, his heart heavy, and started up the dusty street. Suddenly his eyes glazed. There, big as life, was Gillis, Brogan's despicable son. He had just swung off his horse and was walking toward the saloon. *By himself.*

Seth felt a surge of fury. Gillis who had tried to kill him from ambush at least three times was now in front of him.

The time had come for reckoning.

Seth moved toward Gillis.

15

It was sundown and Brogan felt uneasy.

He drew a hard breath and stared grimly at the flaming sky. Honey Creek was not far, and he had every reason to feel good. Mire would be there, and it could be that, by this time, he had put Seth among his ancestors.

In spite of that happy thought, though, he felt rotten. He glanced at Gillis and Allen, who were riding behind him, then at Rosemarie, riding on his left. Something was different about her, something had changed, it was subtle, but there. When he looked at her, she no longer smiled, and when he had occasion to give her a refilled canteen, he squeezed her hand. She gave no response; what she did, in fact, was pull her hand quickly away.

Something had gone wrong.

He ransacked his mind for the reason and finally decided it had to be Lottie, the story of how she died, and what he had done to bring it about. He had told her about it, believing it would prove how deeply he felt. He thought it would flatter her, convince her of his passion. He believed Rosemarie was a silk-and-steel girl, someone to whom a man could tell the truth. He thought it would knock her over, but he had misjudged. You didn't lightly tell a woman that you deliberately caused the death of another. He'd been straight with Rosemarie. Instead of pleasing her, it appalled her.

He glanced at her fine profile. Her chin was set hard, her eyes fixed ahead. It was clear that she had pulled away from him.

Brogan felt a quiver of rage. His impulse was to grab her from her horse, throw her to the ground, tear off her clothes and take her right there. His rage was so strong that chances were if Gillis and Allen had not been there, he'd have done just that. He'd gone through plenty for her, and she led him to believe she wanted what he was offering. Suddenly she reversed herself. He felt mocked, humiliated. He gritted his teeth, trying to get control. It wasn't smart—you never got anywhere with a stampede of rage, you did it with craft and cunning. He'd get her, but not by grabbing; she was not a filly to be grabbed.

He decided that when they got into town, he'd ride to the hotel. Surely she'd want rest after their grueling ride. They'd take a couple of rooms: he'd send Gillis and Allen to look for Mire, find out what was happening. Maybe Seth was already pushing daisies. Yes, he wanted to know about Seth, but his passions were fixed on Rosemarie. He'd get to her room, get things straight. If she had pulled away, then he'd make his move, take what he wanted. Maybe it would cure him of his obsession with the damned filly.

The sky was a huge sheet of flame when they rode into town. They trotted the horses down the broad, main street to the Hotel Honey Creek where Brogan pulled up.

He turned to Allen and Gillis. "You boys relax, mosey around town, see Mire, and find out what's happening. It's been a rough ride and I'm sure Rosemarie would like a bath and some quiet time. We'll reserve some rooms. You boys go ahead."

Allen and Gillis watched them go into the hotel, then

started to ride toward the center of town. As they came abreast of the café, Allen pulled up. "Let's get some real grub, I'm sick to death of jerky. I want a decent steak. How about it?"

Gillis scowled. "Dad said to find Mire, and find out what's happening."

"Yeah, he also said to relax, and that's what I aim to do before I do anything else, eat a decent meal. If you want, you go up to the saloon and see what Mire's been doin'." He went into the café.

Gillis watched him, thought for a moment of joining him, then, knowing his father, decided to go to the saloon and find Mire.

He reached the saloon, dismounted, and started for the steps.

Then he saw the cowboy in the street staring at him. His nerves jumped.

Thunderation, it was Seth!

Honey Creek's main street was bathed in luminous light from the flaming, orange sky overhead. The glow lit the nearby shops along the street—the livery, the café, the merchandise store.

Seth walked slowly toward Gillis, his senses feeling razor sharp. He seemed aware of everything: the sky, the reflection of the sun in the windows of the shops, the mongrel trotting behind a broad-shouldered cowboy whose pinto raised a fine dust.

Most of all, Seth was aware of Gillis who strolled toward the saloon, in a fog, as always, a lunkhead who didn't know what the world was about. He was a chip off the old block, a grasping, greedy yearling. As long as Gillis breathed, Seth felt his life in jeopardy—not from a straight draw but from a sneak attack. He watched the pale, blue eyes when they caught sight of him, the jolt, the sudden anxiety in them.

"Hello, Gillis," he said. "Surprised to see you."

Gillis's mind worked fast. There was no way, he figured, for Seth to know who had fired a shot at him from the crest on the trail into Honey Creek. How could he know?

"Hello, Seth. Whatcha doin' in this town?"

"I was about to ask you that." Seth noted that Gillis wore his gun in a cross holster. "I had the idea you were out at the ranch, managing it." His smile was ironic. "Isn't that what you been doin' lately, managing the ranch?"

Gillis was aware of the irony. "I try, Seth. I put Murph in charge, while . . ." His voice trailed off.

"While you did what?"

Gillis was confused. "What?"

"I mean, Gillis, you came to do something. What would that be?"

Gillis blushed. "Well, I thought I'd go out and meet Dad. I knew he was due back from Tucson."

"With Rosemarie. That right, Gillis?"

Gillis tried to smile. "Yeah, but why should you care? You're through with that jezebel."

Seth frowned. "What'd you call her?"

"Who, Rosemarie?" Gillis's smile was a bit yellow. "She two-timed you, didn't she, Seth?"

Seth shook his head. "I didn't like that name-calling, Gillis."

Gillis was astonished. "Yeah, but she kicked your ass, remember. You don't have to defend her. If a tart did that to me, you can just bet she'd get the back of my hand. You won't find me defendin' her good name."

Seth stared at him. "Won't catch you defendin' anything decent, Gillis."

That startled Gillis, but he felt it smart to bypass it. He felt the danger of being pushed into a corner, and was hoping, by stalling, Mire or one of his gunfighters might show. "Well, if it makes you happy to say that, Seth."

Seth was silent, studying Gillis. "It makes me unhappy, Gillis, to see a man like you crawling the earth."

Gillis stared, pop-eyed.

"How many times have you tried to bushwhack me, Gillis?"

Gillis took a deep breath. So the sonofabitch knew. He had known all the time they'd been talking. He was after a showdown. Beads of sweat showed on Gillis's forehead.

"You can't believe that, Seth. You're talking about your own stepbrother."

"You're bullshit, Gillis. You just shot at me ten miles back. I know you did. We picked up your tracks."

"You're making a big mistake, Seth," Gillis croaked, his glance darting around.

Seth's lip curled with contempt. "You've killed in your time, haven't you, but never once in a straight showdown. That right, Gillis?"

Gillis was silent. It was true, why should a man risk his life unnecessarily, that would be dumb. He cursed himself for not making sure he had killed Seth during the ambush on the trail.

Seth had been watching him closely. "You are one cowardly mutt, Gillis. You've done rotten things. And today you're goin' to pay for them."

"You're makin' a big mistake, Seth, please," Gillis pleaded and went for his holster, hoping to catch Seth off balance.

But Seth knew his man and his gun came out fast and smooth, barking once. The heavy bullet crashed into Gillis, tearing his chest, ripping the bones beneath, slashing his liver. He stumbled back and groaned, his eyes loaded with fear. He twisted in agony, coughed violently, and his body slowly stopped moving.

He died with his eyes open, the fear frozen in them.

The townsfolk who had been sitting or talking on their porches had stopped to watch the confrontation in the street. They knew a showdown in the making; they'd seen plenty. You always knew, from the hostile stance of two men wearing guns, talking hard in the street, that it wouldn't be long before their guns would fire and someone would go down. The townsfolk watched, fascinated to see someone who'd just been alive move into the dreaded state of death. No man would turn away from such a spectacle.

After the shots were fired and Gillis went down, the townsfolk came forward, crowding around to look closely at the defeated one, the dead Gillis.

The gunshot brought the sheriff and his deputies quickly to the scene. The sheriff glanced at Seth, then stared down at Gillis. He turned to a man in the crowd. "What happened, Caleb?"

"A fair draw, sheriff," said Caleb.

Sheriff McCabe grunted, then turned to a deputy. "Tell Coyle to bring his wagon and get this gent up to Boothill." He looked at Seth. "I'm thinkin' this is goin' to start a lot of bloodshed, Seth. This is Brogan's boy, and he's goin' to yell. The best thing to do is get trackin' outa town. I want you to do that right away, Seth. No hard feelings."

Seth looked down at Gillis. "I couldn't feel bad now, no matter what. In case anyone wants to know, I'm ridin' south."

The sheriff nodded gravely. "Reckon someone will want to know. The sooner you and the Brogan boys get outa town, the better I'm goin' to like it."

Seth stepped into the stirrup, swung over the saddle of his

horse, and took a last look at Gillis. One less coyote in the world, he thought. He smiled grimly thinking of Brogan. Gillis wasn't much, but he was all Brogan had, and he'd scream bloody murder. There was pleasure for Seth in the realization of Brogan's pain. Just so he'd know what Seth had felt in loss of his mother.

As he rode south, Seth felt gratified that Brogan was still alive to feel the pain. Brogan would bring Mire after him, no doubt about that. But Slocum and Arne, if they were still breathing, would also pick up his trail. That'd be something. Slocum's presence gave him confidence.

He would not ride to Silver Fork directly. Who knew, if he was lucky enough to get past Mire and Brogan, he might, in the end, reclaim his ranch. The thought elated him.

Then he remembered Mire, the fastest and most feared gunfighter in the territory. His young face creased with anxiety as he rode the twisting trail.

16

In the hour before the showdown between Seth and Gillis, Brogan was resting in his room at the Hotel Honey Creek, his mind focused on a most disturbing idea—Rosemarie.

Brogan looked absently about the room. It wasn't much—a bed, a chair, a washstand, a pitcher of water and a glass, and the window.

He had bought whiskey from the general store and took a long gulp from the bottle. He needed to dampen the rage that seethed in his gut. Just thinking of Rosemarie made him hurt. If only he could burn this filly out of his mind. It was hard to understand why he craved her so much. What was it? The look of her face, the tempting full lips, the long neck, the ripeness of her body. Was it physical or something more? He had never felt such powerful desire about other women, certainly not about Lottie whom he'd married in cold blood because she was the richest widow he knew. No, there was something special about Rosemarie—for him anyway.

And until now he thought he had her. But he had made a grievous mistake—he'd told her too much. He cursed himself for bad judgment—why had he revealed that he had let Lottie die? It had been murder, no two ways about it. If you could save someone's life by doing something, but didn't do it, you committed murder—just as if you had put a knife through her heart. She was just as dead. But he had thought Rosemarie would admire him because he'd done such a desperate deed for *her*. He had misjudged her. He thought she was his kind, someone who wanted the prizes of life and knew the way to get the best things was sometimes by doing the worst things. Maybe, though, Rosemarie wanted the good things, but didn't like what he'd done to get them.

He put the bottle to his mouth. Did it matter? What mattered was that she must belong to him. Yes, he had killed Lottie to get her, and she was part of the deal; it'd be right smart of her to get that clear in her head.

He could hear her moving next door. He gulped another drink, went into the hall, and knocked on her door. There was a long pause, then she opened it and looked at him. It was hard to read her eyes.

"Aren't you goin' to ask me in?"

She hesitated, then opened the door.

"I brought some whiskey. Have a drink to relax." He poured whiskey into a glass.

She took it and drank some.

He sat down and drew a deep breath. She had removed her boots and washed; she looked freshened. His eyes went over the swell of her breast, the curves of her hips, and he smiled.

"Rosemarie, you're probably one of the most beautiful women in Arizona."

A small smile twisted her lips. "Take another drink, Brogan, you'll include Texas."

"Don't need another to say that. It's not the whiskey." He looked at the bed.

"It's good to get out of the saddle," she said.

He walked to the window. "Well, won't be long before

we'll be back at Silver Fork." He grinned. "To start a new life—together." He turned to her. She had that cool, faraway look. He felt the bite of anger, but controlled it.

"What's wrong, Rosemarie?"

"What do you mean?"

"You seem cold. You've pulled away."

She lifted the whiskey, but said nothing.

"I thought you were honest, Rosemarie. Are you?"

She stared. "I'm honest."

"Then tell me what's bothering you."

She looked out the window. "Things are different."

He gritted his teeth. "Different? Listen. I want us to get married. I want to make you a partner. We'll have the biggest and richest ranch. You want that, don't you?"

"No, I think not."

His face reddened. He spoke slowly. "It's because of Lottie, isn't it?"

She faced him, her eyes like blue chips of ice. "How could you let her go through that? Let her die from snake poison. A terrible, agonizing death. You could have saved her."

He clamped his jaw so hard, he thought his teeth might break. Just as he thought, it had been Lottie. He cursed his stupidity. If he'd kept his mouth shut, everyone would think it had been a bad accident, then he'd have her. Had he killed his chances?

"I did it for you, Rosemarie. There'd be no way for us to come together. She'd be there always. Don't you see?"

She shook her head. "You don't kill someone to get someone, Brogan, don't *you* see?"

"It was the only way."

"No, it wasn't. You could have given up the ranch."

He gaped at her. Was she crazy? "Give up Silver Fork? That'd be loco. What would we have? You wouldn't even look at me if I came to you with nothing. Would you?"

"Brogan—I don't know. At least you'd come with clean hands. How can I think of you now? Lottie would always come to mind when you'd come close to me. That's how women are."

His pulse beat hard, he felt consuming rage, despair. He had wanted her so badly that he had killed to get her, and the killing had ruined it all. She stood there, her beautiful face cold, her breasts thrusting against her shirt. Why shouldn't he take her? He'd paid enough.

He moved toward her and she read the gleam in his eyes. She backed away to the open drawer behind her, and a gun appeared in her hands.

Her smile was icy. "I don't believe in force, Brogan. At any time."

He took another step.

She cocked the pistol. "A castrated stallion is never bothered by sex."

He paled. She'd do it. He stepped back. There might be another way. He'd take good care of this bitch. Just a matter of time.

"Okay, Rosemarie. We'll do it your way."

He turned and went out of the room.

She sat on the chair and thought for a few moments. Then she smiled. It was not a nice smile.

Slocum shut the door gently on Annabelle, paused, and smiled. There was nothing so pleasing as easing the natural urgencies of the flesh with the cooperation of a pert filly.

He moved down the stairs into the smoke and noise where cowboys drank, laughed, cursed, and gambled. The whiskey was flowing and men were playing. He scanned the crowd, but did not see Seth, which made him thoughtful.

He wondered if he should mosey outside for a look around. Mire and Seth out on the street could be dangerous if they met.

Then he heard a murmur of excitement at one of the poker tables. There was Lennie sitting in a game with two men, pulling in the pot with a winning hand. Lennie was a muscular gunhawk with piercing, gray eyes in a well-formed face. He seemed keenly aware of Arne who stood with the onlookers. Slocum drifted over and stood alongside Arne. Wouldn't be the first time that a card game could be the come-on for a gundown.

He'd be ready, just in case.

After a break in the game, Lennie looked hard at them. "Come in and play poker, gents. You ain't goin' to get rich standin' there. Gotta play to win."

"Gotta play to lose, too," Slocum said.

Lennie grinned. "You're not afraid?"

Slocum smiled slowly, "Ain't been afraid for a long time."

Lennie studied him. "Wouldn't surprise me. But I'll tell you about winning poker—it's all a matter of nerve."

"Some nerve, some skill, and a lot of luck," Slocum said.

"Winning a bit, Lennie, aren't you?" Arne said.

"A bit, but hope to win more if you gents sit down."

"Why not? It's only money," Slocum said, "and you never know how long you've got to spend it."

Lennie smiled grimly. "That's right, mister. Now that I think of it, Sheehan shoulda spent some money. Too late now."

Slocum and Arne took chairs and played for a while; the cards didn't favor anyone too much. They continued to talk and Slocum couldn't help but think that Lennie wasn't a bad guy, he just mixed with the wrong crowd.

Arne seemed to agree. His craggy face twisted in a smile.

"You don't sound like the kind who'd connect with Mire and his bunch. Why are you totin' a gun for an hombre like Brogan?"

"What do you mean?" asked Lennie.

"He means," said Slocum, "someone like you should have his own ranch, raising cattle and kids. Here you are stickin' your neck out for a no-good hombre like Brogan."

Lennie shrugged. "So he's no good. Who the hell is good? Ain't met that hombre yet."

Arne laughed. "Maybe he's got a point."

Lennie smiled. "And you, Arne? You're stickin' your neck out, too."

Arne shrugged. "I've done plenty of livin'. All I'm good for now is totin' a gun. If I get through this summer, I may settle down, find a piece of land, buy a rockin' chair."

"*If* you get through the summer, but gunfighting is a dangerous occupation, mister." Lennie shuffled the cards and laid them out.

Arne watched the cards thoughtfully. "Yeah, gunfighters don't have much of a future."

Lennie had bad cards and dropped out. He then said, "Tell me this, Slocum, why'd you pull away from Brogan? I figgered you were with us. Now I hear you're not."

Slocum's green eyes glittered. "Brogan is a mean, low-down coyote. I wouldn't take his money."

Lennie grimaced. "Personally, I don't care where the money comes from, long as the payoff is plenty. And Brogan pays."

Slocum shrugged. "Never cared for blood money."

Slocum began to deal, laying out a hole card and four clubs showing for Arne—a possible flush; and two pair of kings and fives for Lennie. Their strong betting forced the other players out. The right hole card for Lennie would mean a full house, the winning hand.

Slocum wondered what would happen if Lennie lost.

Lennie bet fifty dollars. "I'll meet that," Arne said.

Lennie stroked his chin. "You've got nerve, mister. You could lose."

Arne nodded gravely. "You need nerve in this game, didn't you say?"

"You need the right cards, too, and you don't have them," Lennie said. "You could lose."

Arne peeped at his hole card. "You could lose, too."

Lennie wasn't in a hurry, he lit a cigarillo. "It was rough to lose Sheehan. He was a pal. I liked ole Sheehan."

"A lotta good guys are gone," Arne said. "We lost John."

Lennie's gray eyes gleamed strangely. "Here we are playing cards and I'm getting paid to put a man like you in Boothill."

"Yeah, but don't try it," Arne said. He looked thoughtful. "We're not after you, it's Brogan and Gillis."

One of the men who had just joined the onlookers spoke up. "Gillis, you said? Gillis is a goner."

Lennie spoke sharply. "What's that?"

"Happened a while ago. So much noise here, you didn't hear the shot. Gillis is dead as a dodo. A showdown."

"Who shot him?" asked Slocum.

"Seth."

"There you are," said Arne. "One for our side."

"Where's Dick Mire?" Lennie asked quickly.

"He's out there. Might be comin' in."

So Mire was coming, Lennie thought, and here he was playing friendly with this enemy gunman. Mire wouldn't like it, not a bit. In fact, Lennie feared Mire might just jerk his gun and shoot not only Arne but him, too. He'd seen him back in Tombstone shoot two men in one draw.

Lennie looked at Slocum. "This is not your deal. This is between him and me." He turned to Arne, his eyes like ice, looking the gunhawk. "Show your card, mister."

Arne studied Lennie and his jaw hardened and his body tensed. He showed his card—a club—he had a flush. "Looks like a winner."

Lennie showed his card, a five. He had a full house, the winner's hand.

"You lose," said Lennie, standing. He went for his gun, as did Arne, whose draw was a hairbreadth faster. Lennie crashed back over his chair and went down, a bullet in his chest. "Sonofabitch," he muttered, twisting, grabbing at his chest, as if he could dig out the bullet. His head dropped to the floor and he lay still.

Slocum came forward, his jaw hard, he'd been ready to confront Lennie if he had won the draw, but Arne was alive. Seth was alive, too. Gillis was dead, as was Lennie.

Who did Brogan have left? Mire, the Invincible Gun, was left, and Allen, and Brogan himself, the latter, in his own sneaky way, the most dangerous.

What about Rosemarie, where was she?

Things were getting mighty interesting.

17

Brogan heard the shot in his dream.

He had been lying on the bed, his legs sprawled, in a doze. The riding during the day in the hot sun had depleted him and he needed a siesta. He slipped into sleep and was dreaming of himself in fast pursuit of a mysterious rider. The figure ahead was dim, hard to identify, but it seemed a matter of life and death to catch up. As he closed the distance, he felt a jubilant surge; he could perceive the rider was a woman in breeches and boots, but not any woman— it was Rosemarie. He kicked at his mare, moving closer, then, just as he reached out, the figure whipped around and his heart almost stopped from the horror, for it was not the face of Rosemarie, but that of a death head, a grinning skull, with deep, cavernous sockets that glared. It sickened him so, that he reached for his gun, and that's when he heard the shot.

The sound was so realistic it pierced his dream. He came abruptly to a sitting position in the bed, his face bathed in sweat. He listened; there were dim sounds out on the street—that shot was not in his dream. He crawled off the bed, trying to shake the mental cobwebs and looked out the window. There was a crowd around a man on the ground in front of the saloon. A gunfight. He slipped on his gunbelt and clambered down the hotel stairs. He tried to shake the mood of his dream as he walked up the street. He could barely glimpse the man on the ground. Who would it be? Seth, he decided, that hombre was long overdue. Mire or one of his other gunfighters had caught Seth, finally. If that was the case, he was through with that pest, wouldn't have to carry that damn cross.

As he came nearer, he could see more clearly, and the mood of his dream hit him again with sickening sharpness. Suddenly he knew—though he didn't want to know—who lay there.

Gillis!

He rushed forward, pushed men aside, and bent to Gillis who lay there, his eyes unseeing, the blood smeared over his chest. His boy, dead.

He looked around, with fearful eyes, suddenly aware of the townsfolk watching.

"Who shot him?"

"Seth. It was a showdown," said a voice.

Brogan looked at the speaker. It was Sheriff McCabe. "A fair fight, we have witnesses."

Brogan ground his teeth. Gillis had to be forced, he wouldn't pull his gun otherwise. He scrutinized the faces but found none of his men. Where the hell were they? Sheehan, Lennie, Mire? Then he saw Allen coming down the street out of the café, and there was Mire riding in. Gone on a jaunt, when he shoulda been here. He'd bought all those men, and not one had been there to protect his boy. The burial man had come with his wagon and they were putting Gillis on it, to put him in a coffin and bury him in Boothill.

Brogan jaw's hardened. He had told Gillis to stay on the ranch, that it'd be safer, but that boy had never had any common sense. Now he was gone. His only son.

He looked around, his face grim.

"Where's Seth?"

"I told him to leave town," the sheriff said. "He's gone. There's goin' to be no more shootin' in Honey Creek today."

Brogan's voice was hoarse. "It doesn't have to happen in Honey Creek."

Mire and Allen, their faces taut, came up and stood next to Brogan. They watched as Gillis was lifted by two men to the wagon.

Brogan, white-faced, spoke in a hoarse voice. "They shot Gillis." He stared at them viciously. "I pay you boys plenty, but you ain't around to do the job."

Mire looked at him coldly, but decided to say nothing. He had gone to buy dynamite for the buried safe, but he couldn't tell Brogan that. Besides, the hombre was torn with grief. When he simmered down, he'd point out that he had no way of knowing Gillis was in town. Now, looking at Gillis on the wagon, Mire thought that Gillis was destined to catch a bullet sooner than later. He had the viciousness of Brogan, but none of his shrewdness. Gillis was a backshooter and a knothead, destined for a short life. If Seth hadn't shot him down, someone else would have.

Brogan began to follow the burial wagon. Mire looked at Allen, shrugged, and they fell in step behind Brogan.

They were headed for Boothill to bury Gillis.

Twenty minutes later, Slocum and Arne came out of the saloon. By this time most of the crowd had dissipated, but Sheriff McCabe was still there.

"I have a message for you boys," he said, looking at Slocum.

"And what's that?" Slocum was pleasant.

"Your sidekick, Seth, has taken the trail south. He wanted you to know." The sheriff mopped his face with his kerchief. "And to tell you the truth, nuthin' would please me more than for you boys to go after him, quicker n' hell, jest so we can bring some quiet back to this town."

Slocum nodded. "Could I ask—where's Brogan?"

"Gone to bury his boy. So you see, it's a good time to leave. He's got blood in his eye."

"Mire is with him, I reckon?"

The sheriff nodded. "There's one, hot gun." He paused to put his kerchief around his neck. "If I were you, I'd keep a respectful distance from that gent."

Slocum's smile was grim. "Trouble is, he doesn't intend to keep a respectful distance from me." He turned to Arne. "Let's go find Seth."

The sun rose on the horizon, a golden ball, its light smearing the huge, scalloped mountains with bronze. A new day, Seth thought, and before it was over, much could happen.

Seth studied the trail behind him, but could see nothing. They'd be coming sooner or later, he knew that. Certainly Brogan and his gunhawk, Mire, were tailing him. Brogan had to be seething for revenge.

Seth pictured to himself the pain Brogan must have felt at the sight of Gillis, sprawled dead on the dusty street in Honey Creek. Picturing Brogan like that, in some way helped soften the pain he himself still felt at the untimely death of his mother. He still ached about her—his lovely mother who, all his life, had given him care and tenderness.

But there'd be no final score until he had settled with Brogan himself.

His mind skipped to Rosemarie. He remembered how Brogan had fastened on her, a girl he'd been crazy about. How could he know if Brogan had caused his rift with

Rosemarie? Thinking of her turned his mood down. He sure cared for that filly, and could tell his feelings about her hadn't changed. He wondered where she was. By this time, he wondered if she'd discovered Brogan was an oversized four-flusher.

He sighed and rode on until he saw a line hut butted against the hillside. That was a nice, fortified spot; he could rest and survey the oncoming riders. If he was lucky, maybe Slocum and Arne might show, if they'd escaped the wrath of gunfire from Mire's gunmen. Anything could happen.

He thought of Slocum and smiled; there was something about that green-eyed hombre that made him feel good. On the trail to Honey Creek, Slocum had faced gunmen and Apaches—and he was still breathing easy. If Slocum came down that trail, he'd feel better about Brogan and whoever was left of his miserable bunch.

Slocum, riding with Arne, had little trouble following Seth. Seth had taken no evasive action; he rode directly south. Looking at the desolate landscape they were riding through, Slocum couldn't help but wonder what Seth might be thinking traveling alone, knowing Brogan, in a rage about Gillis, would be trailing him and bringing Mire. Slocum imagined that putting Gillis permanently out of action had to make Seth feel good, whatever other miseries dug at him.

Slocum thought about Mire—the sheriff had said it would be smart to keep Mire at a distance, not bad advice. Slocum had seen Mire shoot, and the man had a dazzling draw. In his jaunts around the territories, Slocum had often heard about the fast gun, the legendary gunfighter, but, in his experience, much was just hearsay, imagination, and exaggeration.

He himself, in some places in the territories, also had a

fearful rep, but didn't have the illusion he couldn't be beat. There were faster guns, there had to be, but Slocum worked for one thing, to get the edge.

He placed his holster low, so his hand wouldn't lose a precious split-second reaching the gun. He filed his gun trigger which gave him another split second. He stared into the opponent's eyes, looking for the subtle flicker when the brain sent the command for the hand to draw. All these things put together gave him an edge of split seconds, and it had kept his skin whole, kept him breathing.

He would have a final showdown with Mire, who had the body of a gunfighter and the gift of great reflexes, like Billy the Kid. Mire was a menace, but there was no point worrying until the time of the showdown.

They stopped at a rocky enclave to give the horses rest and make coffee.

As they sat drinking, Arne said, "I expect Brogan will be coming hard after Seth. We oughta keep an eye peeled."

Slocum nodded. "On the trail, you always keep an eye peeled. If you don't it's doomsday."

Arne shrugged. "Been doomsday for a lot of hombres since we started this fracas. Beyer, Sheehan, John, Lefty, Lennie." He raised his cup. "To tell the truth, Slocum, I'm gettin' mighty tired of the ridin', the shootin', and the blood."

Slocum smiled. "Trouble is, it's not a fracas you can quit. You can't ride off into the sunset—the players won't let you."

"Why not?" Arne looked at a distant crag, ageless stones piled high. An eagle flew off, probably from its nest. "If I started to ride north, why should they come after me?"

"Because you've been ridin' with Seth. You're the enemy, part of the bunch who put Sheehan and Lennie in Boothill. Mire ain't going to forget, and sooner or later, you'll run into a gunhawk. You don't know when or where it will happen, but it will."

Arne nodded. "Reckon so. There's a lot of poison in gents like Brogan and Mire."

He sipped his coffee. "It's sad about Lennie. Not a bad guy. I wouldn't have cared if he slipped away and got lost. What bothered me was that he was fighting for a coyote like Brogan just for the money."

Slocum sighed. "Men do lots of dirty stuff for money— it's the way things are."

"A man like Brogan could never buy my gun," said Arne as he stood up to throw away his coffee grinds. Then came the crack of a rifle and Arne stared in amazement at the bloody hole in his chest as he staggered back and fell.

Slocum, whose low position behind the rock gave him shelter, cursed violently and stayed flat, pulling his gun. The shot had come from that distant crag. The bastard had used a Sharps rifle. It had to be Mire, he was that kind of shooter. Slocum, aware his position behind the boulder had given him shelter, looked again at Arne. The heavy bullet had done its job, the light of life was no longer in his eyes.

Slocum cursed again. Only minutes ago, he'd said, "If you don't keep your eye peeled, it's doomsday."

This camp had not been safe.

What could he do? Go after them—it'd be Brogan and Mire—or he could join Seth.

They wanted Seth. They were coming after him.

Yes, he'd join Seth and wait.

Slocum felt a violent rage as he looked down at Arne.

"Well, that takes care of Arne." Mire brought down the heavy Sharps rifle and turned to Brogan. "Maybe Lennie will rest easier in Boothill now."

Brogan stared down at the tiny figure lying flat, then took the field glasses. Now he could clearly see the small, rocky enclave where they had camped, and Arne's body lying flat.

He turned to Mire, his face was still dark with anger. "Yeah, that wipes out one more of them, but it's Seth I'm after. I won't rest easy 'til he's gone."

They had climbed the spur from the thick bottomed crag, leaving Rosemarie and Allen below. He looked down at them, sitting and waiting. Then he stared again at the camp. "Looks like Slocum got away. Too bad you didn't puncture him, Mire. I worry about him."

Mire shrugged. "I would have hit him if he'd been in the sights. But he wasn't. He's a fox, he's not goin' to position himself where he can be picked off."

When they had left Honey Creek, they rode fast on Seth's trail. Brogan, bitter about the death of Gillis, kept pushing hard, so when Mire saw the spur, from where a man could see a long distance down, he surmised it might do some good.

"Let's you and me go up there," he said quietly to Brogan. "We may sight them."

"What then?"

Mire grinned. "I'll do some shootin' with the Sharps."

Brogan told Allen and Rosemarie to stay put; he and Mire would reconnoiter.

When they got up there, Mire pulled the Sharps from its long holster. "For long-distance shooting," he said.

That made Brogan's eyes gleam. "Let's hope you can see something. We're plenty far off."

Mire did see something. Using the field glasses, he saw Arne, but never got a sight on Slocum; he was there, but behind the boulder.

Brogan watched Mire impatiently. "How long you goin'

to look down there?" he demanded, impatient to get after Seth.

Mire threw him a hard look, then raised the sight on the Sharps and took aim. He waited. When Arne stood up, for whatever reason, Mire squeezed the trigger. He saw the jolt as the heavy bullet hit Arne, saw him go down. Mire held his breath, waiting to see if Slocum would rush into target view, but he didn't.

Slocum was foxy, he had figured what happened, and wasn't going to stick his head out.

"All right, we're through here, let's go after Seth," said Brogan.

Mire calmly gazed at him, then started to clean the Sharps.

"No time for that now," Brogan said irritably.

"I want to talk to you, Brogan." Mire's voice was not that of a paid hand, Brogan noted.

"I'm goin' to tell it to you straight, Brogan. Me and Allen have a bit of money buried not five miles from here. I'm aching to get it. This may be the only time."

Brogan scowled. "You goin' to welch on me, Mire?"

"No, I don't do that." Mire's smile was almost vicious. "I don't welch. But I don't want to bypass this money. It's plenty and we're close. It would only mean an hour. We'll catch up with Seth and Slocum by tomorrow." He stopped and grinned viciously. "I want to show Slocum what a fast draw looks like."

"Yeah, that sounds good." Then Brogan scowled. "What about this money—what is it?"

Mire grinned. "That's not your business. It's just there, and me and Allen gotta get it. Nothing so dumb as to have a fortune in your reach and ride past it."

"It's a fortune now, is it?" Brogan's jaw was hard. He knew what that meant. The boys had robbed a bank or a stage and cached the money. Now they were going to the cache. All right, let them go, so long as they came back. Mire would come—he was a rascal, but he had a code, and that was not to turn on the man who hired his gun.

Besides, Brogan was thinking, what could he do to stop Mire? Nothing. A gun like Mire could ask for the moon and get it.

"Go ahead, Mire. Me and Rosemarie will stick on Seth's tracks. We'll move slow. We'll stop and hole up if it gets sticky."

Mire grinned. "We'll pick you up in a couple of hours."

He looked down at Rosemarie. "Don't treat her mean, Brogan. She's a nice girl."

Brogan glowered. "I know how to treat her, Mire. Just hurry."

Mire lit the fuse, and from behind the boulder, watched the fire crawl along the cord until it hit the dynamite lodged in the lock. There was a short, muffled explosion and the lock splintered.

Now the safe could be opened.

He and Allen moved quickly and flung open the iron box. Two bags of gold nuggets. Mire looked at them, lifted the bags. They were heavy.

Allen grinned from ear to ear. "Hey, Mire, we're rich."

"Rich?" Mire stroked his chin. "What do you figger is in there?"

"'Bout a thousand."

Mire looked gloomy. "Tell the truth, Allen, it's not what I expected. We're lucky the other boys ain't here to collect. Be real trouble."

"Dunno, Mire, seems plenty to me. Lots of things you can do with a thousand."

Mire was still glum, which mystified Allen. "What's the

matter, Mire? You oughta be happy."

"I'm sorry, not your fault, Allen, that this ain't enough for two hombres. One maybe, but not two."

That jolted Allen. He got a hard premonition. "Hey, Mire, you ain't goin' to make the money a big thing, are you?"

Mire shook his head sorrowfully. "Money *is* a big thing, Allen. And we ain't got much time. They're waitin' for me."

Allen got the idea quick enough. Mire didn't care to share a lousy thousand. He was greedy. Chances were, if the others had been alive, it might stop him, but there was no way Mire would share this loot.

"Hey, Mire," Allen said. "You've got Seth and Slocum out there. You're goin' to need all the help you can get."

"No, I ain't," Mire said, glumly.

Allen stared at him and his hand flashed to his holster, but it was too late. The bullet speared his head.

Mire shook his head sadly and muttered, "Never knew what hit him. It was the least I could do for poor Allen."

It was high noon when he caught up with Brogan and Rosemarie.

Brogan stared at him. "Where the hell is Allen?"

Mire shrugged sadly. "He just took his share of the money and rode off. Figured he was rich now, didn't need to work anymore."

Brogan scowled. "And you let him?"

For a moment Mire looked sorrowful. "A man's gotta do what he's gotta do. As for me, I don't forget my obligations." He grinned cheerfully at Rosemarie. "Here I am, ready to help—anyway I can."

Brogan glared. "Yeah, well, let's get goin'. We've got a job."

18

From the high rise, Slocum could see Brogan, Mire, and Rosemarie coming down, riding hard. They had been hot on his trail.

Just ahead of him was the hut. Slocum had looked at the tracks that led to the hut. There was little doubt that Seth was lodged in there. But he had to be careful, Seth could shoot by mistake.

So Slocum crawled up behind the boulders facing the hut. "Don't shoot, it's Slocum."

There was a curse, then Seth opened the shutter.

"Damn you, Slocum. Come in."

Slocum came up fast into the open door. "They're comin'."

Seth rubbed his cheek. "How many?"

"Mire, Brogan, and Rosemarie."

"That's all? What happened?"

"They got whittled down. Who cares how."

"So Rosemarie's comin', too?"

"Yeah, but I don't think she's on his side."

Seth brooded. "She's not? Figger she found out by this time he's a four-flusher?"

"Yup."

"So why's she comin' with him?"

Slocum gazed out the window. "I don't know. Maybe she's comin' for you. Maybe she's comin' because she's forced."

Seth shook his head. "It ain't because of me."

"You never know. A woman is a puzzling creature."

Seth looked out the window. "Well—whatever, we'll know soon enough. They're out there."

Slocum watched them riding single file, Mire in front, Rosemarie in the middle, Brogan behind. They kept riding, and for a moment Slocum wondered if they would ride within gun range, but Mire was not stupid. He stopped, talked to Brogan, then laughed. They dismounted and crawled behind the boulders.

Mire called out. "Hey, Seth. You can't stay in there. You'll run out of water and food. Gotta come out."

Seth scowled. "Whyn't you come in? You're a brave hombre."

"I'm a rich hombre, Seth. Lots of gold. Ain't goin' to risk my life, now that I'm rich, but you better come out. Otherwise, I fear Brogan will do a mischief to your lady."

"She ain't my lady."

Mire grinned. "She thinks she's your lady. Don't want anything to do with Brogan. And he ain't pleased."

Rosemarie suddenly called out. "Seth, Slocum. They're holding me against my will. Come out and kill these rotten dogs."

Brogan slapped her face, hard.

Seth winced and turned to Slocum beside him. "Is this real?"

Slocum had been studying them. "It's real."

"What do you want?" Seth called.

"We have a showdown," Mire said.

"I'll showdown with Brogan," Seth said.

Mire grinned. "I fear that Brogan wants you dead because

of Gillis. He wants me to do it."

"Brogan's got no guts," Seth snarled. "Just the guts to do women, to hit them, or kill them."

Brogan turned to Rosemarie and ripped off her blouse. Her full breasts were exposed. As she tried to hit him, he threw her to the ground and stared with ferocious eyes. "I've been wantin' you for a long time, and I'm goin' to take you right now, behind that rock." He turned and laughed. "After I do it, maybe Seth, that yellow dog in there, will come out."

Mire laughed. "You wouldn't do that, Brogan."

"Oh, yes, I would. I been craving this creature a long time. Now's the payoff."

There was a long silence.

Then Slocum called. "Hey, Mire. I'm glad to hear you're rich. You don't need this bastard, Brogan, anymore. I got a proposition."

"What's that?"

"You and me have a showdown. See who's best. I know you achin' to find that out, but you've got to do us a favor first. Shoot Brogan."

Mire laughed. "Why should I do that?"

"Figure it this way. You get rid of him, then, if you beat me, you've got Rosemarie. I know you been craving her on the sly. Ain't that right?"

Mire's eyes glazed. He threw a quick glance at Rosemarie, at her beautiful breasts, her full figure, her lovely face. "Damn," he said, "you've hit the bull's-eye, Slocum."

He turned, hard-faced, to Brogan. "Pull your gun, Brogan."

"Are you crazy, Mire?"

Mire studied him. "Brogan, I never liked you. Seth's right. You're the kind who likes to do women. I don't mind you being a bastard, but I hate a man who abuses women.

Now, pull your gun. I'll give you one second."

Brogan's face turned purple. "You ungrateful mutt," he snarled, and grabbed at his gun. Mire seemed to watch him for two beats before he moved, a streak of lightning. The bullet hit Brogan and he hurled back and fell, faceup, his hand grabbing his chest, his face distorted with pain and hate.

His gaze slipped to Rosemarie, to Mire. Then, to his amazement, he found himself looking at Slocum, who had come out of the hut and walked over to him. He was standing, watching his death throes.

He felt life flowing out of him with his heart's blood, and for one strange moment he remembered Lottie, Seth's mother. Suddenly, he thought, *I shoulda shot that damned snake*.

Then he died.

Slocum turned to Mire. "That was a decent thing to do. You ain't all that bad. But you're bad enough."

Mire smiled. "Yeah, Slocum. Reckon I'm bad, but that's the way of the world. I liked your proposition of a show-down." His eyes narrowed as he thought for a moment. "I might let you go your ways, you and Seth. Got no real quarrel with either of you, but Rosemarie sticks with me."

Slocum looked at Rosemarie, who had covered her breasts with her hands. Her eyes blazed as she waited for him to speak.

"I'm afraid we can't let that happen, Mire. She asked us to come out and kill you both."

Mire shook his head. "Do you really think you can do that, Slocum? Okay, to tell the truth, it's been in my mind to show you what a fast draw can really look like. I know you're good, I've heard plenty about you. Let's find out who's best."

Slocum nodded.

They walked away from the dead Brogan to flat ground and faced each other. The sun had slipped down and now the sky glowed with gorgeous hues of orange and yellow, gilding the distant mountain. A soft, fragrant breeze stirred the grass. It was not a good day for dying.

They looked at each other.

Seth came out of the hut and started toward them. Mire held up his hand warningly. It stopped Seth in his tracks. He would watch from there.

Slocum studied Mire. He could see no fear; Mire had won too many gunfights and he wasn't nervous now. He expected to win. Slocum felt keyed up. He was facing a top gunfighter, one of the best.

Slocum knew the signal trick in the eyes, when the brain gave the command to move. He studied Mire. He was aware that Mire, too, watched him with fierce intensity. Did he know that eye trick, too?

Nobody moved, the sky flamed, the grass swayed in the breeze, then Slocum saw it, the eye flicker. They both moved, a brilliant display of top gunfighters at their best—smooth, perfect, no waste, all speed, flawless coordination of muscle and eye. They both reached their guns at the same time and brought them up, but Slocum's shaved hair-trigger gave him the imperceptible edge, and his bullet hit Mire in the center of his forehead even as Mire's gun fired—wild.

Mire dropped, his face unchanged. He died, never knowing that he'd been second best.

Seth came running toward Slocum, as did Rosemarie.

Rosemarie caught Seth by the hand and stared into his eyes. "Brogan was a mistake. Seth, I want you back." She leaned toward him. "Do you want me?"

He looked at her and shivered. "I want you," he said.

Rosemarie smiled broadly, then looked at Slocum, her eyes glowing.

"Do you mind, Seth, if I kiss Slocum?"

He laughed. "I swear, if I was a woman, I'd kiss him, too."

GILES TIPPETTE

Author of the best-selling WILSON YOUNG SERIES, BAD NEWS, and CROSS FIRE is back with his most exciting Western adventure yet!

JAILBREAK

Time is running out for Justa Williams, owner of the Half-Moon Ranch in West Texas. His brother Norris is being held in a Mexican jail, and neither bribes nor threats can free him.

Now with the help of a dozen kill-crazy Mexican *banditos,* Justa aims to blast Norris out. But the worst is yet to come: a hundred-mile chase across the Mexican desert with fifty *federales* in hot pursuit.

The odds of reaching the Texas border are a million to nothing . . . and if the Williams brothers don't watch their backs, the road to freedom could turn into the road to hell!

JAILBREAK
by
Giles Tippette

On sale now, wherever Jove Books are sold!

Here is the first chapter
from this new
Western adventure

At supper Norris, my middle brother, said, "I think we got some trouble on that five thousand acres down on the border near Laredo."

He said it serious, which is the way Norris generally says everything. I quit wrestling with the steak Buttercup, our cook, had turned into rawhide and said, "What are you talking about? How could we have trouble on land lying idle?"

He said, "I got word from town this afternoon that a telegram had come in from a friend of ours down there. He says we got some kind of squatters taking up residence on the place."

My youngest brother, Ben, put his fork down and said, incredulously, "*That* five thousand acres? Hell, it ain't nothing but rocks and cactus and sand. Why in hell would anyone want to squat on that worthless piece of nothing?"

Norris just shook his head. "I don't know. But that's what the telegram said. Came from Jack Cole. And if anyone ought to know what's going on down there it would be him."

I thought about it and it didn't make a bit of sense. I was Justa Williams, and my family, my two brothers and myself and our father, Howard, occupied a considerable ranch called the Half-Moon down along the Gulf of Mexico in Matagorda County, Texas. It was some of the best grazing land in the state and we had one of the best herds of purebred and crossbred cattle in that part of the country. In short we were pretty well-to-do.

But that didn't make us any the less ready to be stolen from, if indeed that was the case. The five thousand acres Norris had been talking about had come to us through a trade our father had made some years before. We'd never made any use of the land, mainly because, as Ben had said, it was pretty worthless and because it was a good two hundred miles from our ranch headquarters. On a few occasions we'd bought cattle in Mexico and then used the acreage to hold small groups on while we made up a herd. But other than that, it lay mainly forgotten.

I frowned. "Norris, this doesn't make a damn bit of sense. Right after supper send a man into Blessing with a return wire for Jack asking him if he's certain. What the hell kind of squatting could anybody be doing on that land?"

Ben said, "Maybe they're raisin' watermelons." He laughed.

I said, "They could raise melons, but there damn sure wouldn't be no water in them."

Norris said, "Well, it bears looking into." He got up, throwing his napkin on the table. "I'll go write out that telegram."

I watched him go, dressed, as always, in his town clothes. Norris was the businessman in the family. He'd been sent down to the University at Austin and had got considerable learning about the ins and outs of banking and land deals and all the other parts of our business that didn't directly involve the ranch. At the age of twenty-nine I'd been the boss of the operation a good deal longer than I cared to think about. It had been thrust upon me by our father when I wasn't much more than twenty. He'd said he wanted me to take over while he was still strong enough to help me out of my mistakes and I reckoned that was partly true. But it had just seemed that after our mother had died the life had sort of gone out of him. He'd been one of the earliest settlers, taking up the land not long after Texas had become a republic in 1845. I figured all the years of fighting Indians and then Yankees and scalawags and carpetbaggers and cattle thieves had taken their toll on him. Then a few years back he'd been nicked in the lungs by a bullet that should never have been allowed to head his way and it had thrown an extra strain on his heart. He was pushing seventy and he still had plenty of head on his shoulders, but mostly all he did now was sit around in his rocking chair and stare out over the cattle and land business he'd built. Not to say that I didn't go to him for advice when the occasion demanded. I did, and mostly I took it.

Buttercup came in just then and sat down at the end of the table with a cup of coffee. He was near as old as Dad and almost completely worthless. But he'd been one of the first hands that Dad had hired and he'd been kept on even after he couldn't sit a horse anymore. The problem was he'd elected himself cook, and that was the sorriest day our family had ever seen. There were two Mexican women hired to cook for the twelve riders we kept full-time, but Buttercup insisted on cooking for the family.

Mainly, I think, because he thought he was one of the family. A notion we could never completely dissuade him from.

So he sat there, about two days of stubble on his face, looking as scrawny as a pecked-out rooster, sweat running down his face, his apron a mess. He said, wiping his forearm across his forehead, "Boy, it shore be hot in there. You boys shore better be glad you ain't got no business takes you in that kitchen."

Ben said, in a loud mutter, "I wish you didn't either."

Ben, at twenty-five, was easily the best man with a horse or a gun that I had ever seen. His only drawback was that he was hotheaded and he tended to act first and think later. That ain't a real good combination for someone that could go on the prod as fast as Ben. When I had argued with Dad about taking over as boss, suggesting instead that Norris, with his education, was a much better choice, Dad had simply said, "Yes, in some ways. But he can't handle Ben. You can. You can handle Norris, too. But none of them can handle you."

Well, that hadn't been exactly true. If Dad had wished it I would have taken orders from Norris even though he was two years younger than me. But the logic in Dad's line of thinking had been that the Half-Moon and our cattle business was the lodestone of all our businesses and only I could run that. He had been right. In the past I'd imported purebred Whiteface and Hereford cattle from up North, bred them to our native Longhorns and produced cattle that would bring twice as much at market as the horse-killing, all-bone, all-wild Longhorns. My neighbors had laughed at me at first, claiming those square little purebreds would never make it in our Texas heat. But they'd been wrong and, one by one, they'd followed the example of the Half-Moon.

Buttercup was setting up to take off on another one of his long-winded harangues about how it had been in the "old days" so I quickly got up, excusing myself, and went into the big office we used for sitting around in as well as a place of business. Norris was at the desk composing his telegram so I poured myself out a whiskey and sat down. I didn't want to hear about any trouble over some worthless five thousand acres of borderland. In fact I didn't want to hear about any troubles of any kind. I was just two weeks short of getting married, married to a lady I'd been courting off and on for five years, and I was mighty anxious that nothing come up to interfere with our plans. Her name was Nora Parker and her daddy owned and run the general mercantile in our nearest town, Blessing. I'd almost lost her once before to a Kansas City drummer. She'd finally gotten tired of waiting on me, waiting until the ranch didn't occupy all my time, and almost run off with a smooth-talking Kansas City drummer that called on her daddy in the harness trade. But she'd come to her senses in time and got off the train in Texarkana and returned home.

But even then it had been a close thing. I, along with my men and brothers and help from some of our neighbors, had been involved with stopping a huge herd of illegal cattle being driven up from Mexico from crossing our range and infecting our cattle with tick fever which could have wiped us all out. I tell you it had been a bloody business. We'd lost four good men and had to kill at least a half dozen on the other side. Fact of the business was I'd come about as close as I ever had to getting killed myself, and that was going some for the sort of rough-and-tumble life I'd led.

Nora had almost quit me over it, saying she just couldn't take the uncertainty. But in the end, she'd stuck by me. That had been the year before, 1896, and I'd convinced her that civilized law was coming to the country, but until it did, we that had been there before might have to take things into our own hands from time to time.

She'd seen that and had understood. I loved her and she loved me and that was enough to overcome any of the trouble we were still likely to encounter from day to day.

So I was giving Norris a pretty sour look as he finished his telegram and sent for a hired hand to ride it into Blessing, seven miles away. I said, "Norris, let's don't make a big fuss about this. That land ain't even crossed my mind in at least a couple of years. Likely we got a few Mexican families squatting down there and trying to scratch out a few acres of corn."

Norris gave me his businessman's look. He said, "It's our land, Justa. And if we allow anyone to squat on it for long enough or put up a fence they can lay claim. That's the law. My job is to see that we protect what we have, not give it away."

I sipped at my whiskey and studied Norris. In his town clothes he didn't look very impressive. He'd inherited more from our mother than from Dad so he was not as wide-shouldered and slim-hipped as Ben and me. But I knew him to be a good, strong, dependable man in any kind of fight. Of course he wasn't that good with a gun, but then Ben I weren't all that good with books like he was. But I said, just to jolly him a bit, "Norris, I do believe you are running to suet. I may have to put you out with Ben working the horse herd and work a little of that fat off you."

Naturally it got his goat. Norris had always envied Ben and me a little. I was just over six foot and weighed right around a hundred and ninety. I had inherited my daddy's big hands and big shoulders. Ben was almost a copy of me except he was about a size smaller. Norris said, "I weigh the same as I have for the last five years. If it's any of your business."

I said, as if I was being serious, "Must be them sack suits you wear. What they do, pad them around the middle?"

He said, "Why don't you just go to hell."

After he'd stomped out of the room I got the bottle of whiskey and an extra glass and went down to Dad's room. It had been one of his bad days and he'd taken to bed right after lunch. Strictly speaking he wasn't supposed to have no whiskey, but I watered him down a shot every now and then and it didn't seem to do him no harm.

He was sitting up when I came in the room. I took a moment to fix him a little drink, using some water out of his pitcher, then handed him the glass and sat down in the easy chair by the bed. I told him what Norris had reported and asked what he thought.

He took a sip of his drink and shook his head. "Beats all I ever heard," he said. "I took that land in trade for a bad debt some fifteen, twenty years ago. I reckon I'd of been money ahead if I'd of hung on to the bad debt. That land won't even raise weeds, well as I remember, and Noah was in on the last rain that fell on the place."

We had considerable amounts of land spotted around the state as a result of this kind of trade or that. It was Norris's business to keep up with their management. I was just bringing this to Dad's attention more out of boredom and impatience for my wedding day to arrive than anything else.

I said, "Well, it's a mystery to me. How you feeling?"

He half smiled. "Old." Then he looked into his glass. "And I never liked watered whiskey. Pour me a dollop of the straight stuff in here."

I said, "Now, Howard. You know—"

He cut me off. "If I wanted somebody to argue with I'd send for Buttercup. Now do like I told you."

I did, but I felt guilty about it. He took the slug of whiskey down in one pull. Then he leaned his head back on the pillow and said, "Aaaaah. I don't give a damn what that horse doctor says, ain't nothing makes a man feel as good inside as a shot of the best."

I felt sorry for him laying there. He'd always led just the kind of life he wanted—going where he wanted, doing what he wanted, having what he set out to get. And now he was reduced to being a semi-invalid. But one thing that showed the strength that was still in him was that you *never* heard him complain. He said, "How's the cattle?"

I said, "They're doing all right, but I tell you we could do with a little of Noah's flood right now. All this heat and no rain is curing the grass off way ahead of time. If it doesn't let up we'll be feeding hay by late September, early October. And that will play hell on our supply. Could be we won't have enough to last through the winter. Norris thinks we ought to sell off five hundred head or so, but the market is doing poorly right now. I'd rather chance the weather than take a sure beating by selling off."

He sort of shrugged and closed his eyes. The whiskey was relaxing him. He said, "You're the boss."

"Yeah," I said. "Damn my luck."

I wandered out of the back of the house. Even though it was nearing seven o'clock of the evening it was still good and hot. Off in the distance, about a half a mile away, I could see the outline of the house I was building for Nora and myself. It was going to be a close thing to get it finished by our wedding day. Not having any riders to spare for the project, I'd imported a building contractor from Galveston, sixty miles away. He'd arrived with a half a dozen Mexican laborers and a few skilled masons and they'd set up a little tent city around the place. The contractor had gone back to Galveston to fetch some materials, leaving his Mexicans behind. I walked along idly, hoping he wouldn't forget that the job wasn't done. He had some of my money, but not near what he'd get when he finished the job.

Just then Ray Hays came hurrying across the back lot toward me. Ray was kind of a special case for me. The only problem with that was that he knew it and wasn't a bit above taking advantage of the situation. Once, a few years past, he'd saved my life by going against an evil man that he was working for at the time, an evil man who meant to have my life. In gratitude I'd given Ray a good job at the Half-Moon, letting him work directly under Ben, who was responsible for the horse herd. He was a good, steady man and a good man with a gun. He was also fair company. When he wasn't talking.

He came churning up to me, mopping his brow. He said, "Lordy, boss, it is—"

I said, "Hays, if you say it's hot I'm going to knock you down."

He gave me a look that was a mixture of astonishment and hurt. He said, "Why, whatever for?"

I said, "*Everybody* knows it's hot. Does every son of a bitch you run into have to make mention of the fact?"

His brow furrowed. "Well, I never thought of it that way. I 'spect you are right. Goin' down to look at yore house?"

I shook my head. "No. It makes me nervous to see how far they've got to go. I can't see any way it'll be ready on time."

He said, "Miss Nora ain't gonna like that."

I gave him a look. "I guess you felt forced to say that."

He looked down. "Well, maybe she won't mind."

I said, grimly, "The hell she won't. She'll think I did it a-purpose."

"Aw, she wouldn't."

"Naturally you know so much about it, Hays. Why don't you tell me a few other things about her."

"I was jest tryin' to lift yore spirits, boss."

I said, "You keep trying to lift my spirits and I'll put you on the haying crew."

He looked horrified. No real cowhand wanted any work he couldn't do from the back of his horse. Haying was a hot, hard, sweaty job done either afoot or from a wagon seat. We generally brought in contract Mexican labor to handle ours. But I'd been known in the past to discipline a cowhand by giving him a few days on the hay gang. Hays said, "Boss, now I never meant nothin'. I swear. You know me, my mouth gets to runnin' sometimes. I swear I'm gonna watch it."

I smiled. Hays always made me smile. He was so easily buffaloed. He had it soft at the Half-Moon and he knew it and didn't want to take any chances on losing a good thing.

I lit up a cigarillo and watched dusk settle in over the coastal plains. It wasn't but three miles to Matagorda Bay and it was quiet enough I felt like I could almost hear the waves breaking on the shore. Somewhere in the distance a mama cow bawled for her calf. The spring crop were near about weaned by now, but there were still a few mamas that wouldn't cut the apron strings. I stood there reflecting on how peaceful things had been of late. It suited me just fine. All I wanted was to get my house finished, marry Nora and never handle another gun so long as I lived.

The peace and quiet were short-lived. Within twenty-four hours we'd had a return telegram from Jack Cole. It said:

YOUR LAND OCCUPIED BY TEN TO TWELVE MEN STOP
CAN'T BE SURE WHAT THEY'RE DOING BECAUSE THEY
RUN STRANGERS OFF STOP APPEAR TO HAVE A GOOD
MANY CATTLE GATHERED STOP APPEAR TO BE FENCING
STOP ALL I KNOW STOP

I read the telegram twice and then I said, "Why this is crazy as hell! That land wouldn't support fifty head of cattle."

We were all gathered in the big office. Even Dad was there, sitting in his rocking chair. I looked up at him. "What do you make of this, Howard?"

He shook his big, old head of white hair. "Beats the hell out of me, Justa. I can't figure it."

Ben said, "Well, I don't see where it has to be figured. I'll take five men and go down there and run them off. I don't care what they're doing. They ain't got no business on our land."

I said, "Take it easy, Ben. Aside from the fact you don't need to be getting into any more fights this year, I can't spare you or five men. The way this grass is drying up we've got to keep drifting those cattle."

Norris said, "No, Ben is right. We can't have such affairs going on with our property. But we'll handle it within the law. I'll simply take the train down there, hire a good lawyer and have the matter settled by the sheriff. Shouldn't take but a few days."

Well, there wasn't much I could say to that. We couldn't very well let people take advantage of us, but I still hated to be without Norris's services even for a few days. On matters other than the ranch he was the expert, and it didn't seem like there was a day went by that some financial question didn't come up that only he could answer. I said, "Are you sure you can spare yourself for a few days?"

He thought for a moment and then nodded. "I don't see why not. I've just moved most of our available cash into short-term municipal bonds in Galveston. The market is looking all right and everything appears fine at the bank. I can't think of anything that might come up."

I said, "All right. But you just keep this in mind. You are not a gun hand. You are not a fighter. I do not want you going anywhere near those people, whoever they are. You do it legal and let the sheriff handle the eviction. Is that understood?"

He kind of swelled up, resenting the implication that he couldn't handle himself. The biggest trouble I'd had through the years when trouble had come up had been keeping Norris out of it. Why he couldn't just be content to be a wagon load of brains was more than I could understand. He said, "Didn't you just hear me say I intended to go through a lawyer and the sheriff? Didn't I just say that?"

I said, "I wanted to be sure you heard yourself."

He said, "Nothing wrong with my hearing. Nor my approach to this matter. You seem to constantly be taken with the idea that I'm always looking for a fight. I think you've got the wrong brother. I use logic."

"Yeah?" I said. "You remember when that guy kicked you in the balls when they were holding guns on us? And then we chased them twenty miles and finally caught them?"

He looked away. "That has nothing to do with this."

"Yeah?" I said, enjoying myself. "And here's this guy, shot all to hell. And what was it you insisted on doing?"

Ben laughed, but Norris wouldn't say anything.

I said, "Didn't you insist on us standing him up so you could kick him in the balls? Didn't you?"

He sort of growled, "Oh, go to hell."

I said, "I just want to know where the logic was in that."

He said, "Right is right. I was simply paying him back in kind. It was the only thing his kind could understand."

I said, "That's my point. You just don't go down there and go to paying back a bunch of rough hombres in kind. Or any other currency for that matter."

That made him look over at Dad. He said, "Dad, will you make him quit treating me like I was ten years old? He does it on purpose."

But he'd appealed to the wrong man. Dad just threw his hands in the air and said, "Don't come to me with your troubles. I'm just a boarder around here. You get your orders from Justa. You know that."

Of course he didn't like that. Norris had always been a strong hand for the right and wrong of a matter. In fact, he may have been one of the most stubborn men I'd ever met. But he didn't say anything, just gave me a look and muttered something about hoping a mess came up at the bank while he was gone and then see how much boss I was.

But he didn't mean nothing by it. Like most families, we fought amongst ourselves and, like most families, God help the outsider who tried to interfere with one of us.

A special offer for people who enjoy reading the best Westerns published today. If you enjoyed this book, subscribe now and get . . .

TWO FREE

A $5.90 VALUE—NO OBLIGATION

If you enjoyed this book and would like to read more of the very best Westerns being published today, you'll want to subscribe to True Value's Western Home Subscription Service. If you enjoyed the book you just read and want more of the most exciting, adventurous, action packed Westerns, subscribe now.

Each month the editors of True Value will select the 6 very best Westerns from America's leading publishers for special readers like you. You'll be able to preview these new titles as soon as they are published, FREE for ten days with no obligation.

TWO FREE BOOKS

When you subscribe, we'll send you your first month's shipment of the newest and best 6 Westerns for you to preview. With your first shipment, two of these books will be yours as our introductory gift to you absolutely FREE, regardless of what you decide to do. If you like them, as much as we think you will, keep all six books but pay for just 4 at the low subscriber rate of just $2.45 each. If you decide to return them, keep 2 of the titles as our gift. No obligation.

Special Subscriber Savings

When you become a True Value subscriber you'll save money several ways. First, all regular monthly selections will be billed at the low subscriber price of just $2.45 each. That's

WESTERNS!

at least a savings of $3.00 each month below the publishers price. Second, there is never any shipping, handling or other hidden charges—Free home delivery. What's more there is no minimum number of books you must buy, you may return any selection for full credit and you can cancel your subscription at any time. A TRUE VALUE!

Mail the coupon below

To start your subscription and receive 2 FREE WESTERNS, fill out the coupon below and mail it today. We'll send your first shipment which includes 2 FREE BOOKS as soon as we receive it.